Vic Evans was born in Wrexham and grew up in the town and on his aunt's hill farm in North Wales. Having worked in the aircraft industry and in engineering for twenty-nine years and taught in secondary schools for a further twenty years, Vic turned his hand to writing fiction. His first novel, *Miriam*, was inspired by his own family history as well as by the recollections of Wrexham men who fought in the Spanish Civil War. *Murder in the Welsh Hills,* his second novel, is a tense and gripping political thriller set in the rugged landscape of Llangollen.

Vic Evans lives on the Kent coast and he has three children and four grandchildren.

Also by Vic Evans and available from Headline Accent

Miriam

MURDER
IN THE
WELSH HILLS

Vic Evans

ACCENT

First published in 2020 by Headline Accent
An imprint of HEADLINE PUBLISHING GROUP

5

Cataloguing in Publication Data is available from the British Library

ISBN 978 1 7861 5690 7

Typeset in 10.5/13pt Bembo Std by Jouve (UK), Milton Keynes

Printed and bound in Great Britain by Clays Ltd, Elcograf S.p.A.

Headline's policy is to use papers that are natural, renewable and recyclable
products and made from wood grown in well-managed forests and other
controlled sources. The logging and manufacturing processes are expected
to conform to the environmental regulations of the country of origin.

HEADLINE PUBLISHING GROUP
An Hachette UK Company
Carmelite House
50 Victoria Embankment
London
EC4Y 0DZ

www.headline.co.uk
www.hachette.co.uk

To the memory of
Marie Evans (1932–2016)
of Llangollen and Bwlchgwyn

Chapter One

Moscow, Friday 23rd July 1993
Office of the Deputy Prime Minister of the
Russian Federation, Mikhail Poltoranin

The splintering crash as the hinges of the door were torn out of its frame in response to the single blow of the sledgehammer brought Poltoranin to his feet. His two assistants scurried into the inner office. The wielder of the sledgehammer stood modestly to one side, allowing two large dark-suited men to enter. Poltoranin's assistants stole out behind them. The two men came round to him, seized his arms and thrust him face-down on his desk top. Another slightly built man appeared through the wrecked door. He advanced with a bearing indicating he was obviously in charge. Clutching a handful of Poltoranin's hair and wrenching his head up with one hand, he thrust a document before his eyes with the other. Putting his mouth to his ear, he said in a sibilant voice that turned Poltoranin's blood cold, 'Deputy Prime Minister, this is a search warrant issued by Chief Prosecutor Stepankov. I'm the investigator in command of this group and we've come to exercise it.'

He snatched the document away and stuffed it in his jacket pocket, leaving his hands free to grasp Poltoranin's ears and pull his head close to his own heavily pock-marked face. 'It is a corruption investigation, Poltoranin,' he snarled, 'aimed at the highest level of government. Do you understand?'

Poltoranin blanched at the blast of garlicky breath and was slow to answer until the hold on his ears was eased.

1

'Well?' demanded the investigator.

Poltoranin would have nodded if his ears had been free but instead he managed a mumbled, '*Da.*'

'In a moment we're going to release you and you are going over to the safe to open it and unlock all drawers and containers. Is that clear?' The investigator emphasised each word of his question by pulling Poltoranin's head up and down by his ears.

Poltoranin attempted a painful nod but instead made do with an affirming grunt.

'Then you're going to assist us,' the investigator went on, 'as we go through each file in this office, turning the place inside out making sure nothing is missed or, as we say, "accidentally lost". You will do this voluntarily, in a spirit of cooperation. Agreed?'

He grunted again.

'Good.'

As his arms were released, Poltoranin moved towards the red telephone on his desk but the investigator was there before him, placing a well-manicured hand over it. 'If you're thinking of contacting your friend Yeltsin,' he sneered, 'you're wasting your time. He's taking a short holiday in the countryside and he's not to be disturbed.'

Extract from *The Scotsman* newspaper, 23rd July 1993:

Today in Moscow, prosecutors armed with a search warrant entered the office of Deputy Prime Minister Mikhail Poltoranin, 53, a close friend of President Yeltsin, seizing KGB documents transferred from the Kremlin on Yeltsin's orders. Poltoranin told reporters he voluntarily opened his office and gave the team of investigators all the documents they requested. He claimed he wasn't arrested but he was shaken by the four-hour search. 'These outrageous methods are frightening,' he said.

It seems Russia's chief prosecutor Valentin Stepankov has sided with the legislature against Yeltsin and launched a corruption investigation aimed at the upper echelon of government. The investigator who led the search said he was looking for documents about the Berlin Friendship House, *a former so-called Soviet cultural centre in the eastern part of the city.*

Chapter Two

Llangollen, North Wales February 1956

Mary got up from her knees. She put down the scrubbing brush. Arching her back she placed her hands firmly on the base of her spine to ease the stiffness as she watched little Huw playing with his green and red wooden train.

Huw's sleep had been disturbed. He was at an age too young for school but old enough to absorb ideas and images that untangled in sleep, giving him nightmares. Although he did not have the language to describe them to his parents it was clear they contained features from his cloth book: a clown; a giant; and a witch with enormous eyes. The nightmares had ranged throughout the night and several times Mary had left Owain in bed to go to him, leaving her tired. Eventually they had taken him into their own bed. Something they would never have done with the others, but Huw was different.

There were thirteen years between Gwen, who'd been the youngest, and Huw. Mary was forty-five when he was born. The boys were twenty and seventeen, not yet married and still living at home. Huw had come into their lives like a beam of bright unexpected sunshine. The house was transformed. Owain had always treated the others with reserve and maintained an air of gravity in his relations with them. With Huw, it was different. Owain could not bear to be separated from him, asking about him as soon as he set foot over the threshold when he came home from work. His reserve disappeared with him doing roly-polies on the mat, making comical noises and

3

burying his face in Huw's belly as he squealed and wriggled. The others would watch these antics for hours, sometimes joining in. There was always one of them playing with him and helping to dress him, wondering at the perfection of his dimpled little limbs as they eased them into sleeves and trouser legs.

Mary tore her attention away from Huw. There was work to be done. The water in the bucket had become cool and dirty. Time to empty it and fill with more from the heater. The heater was a metal box that was part of the range. It was kept full from the top of the hob and the fire in the grate kept it at a high temperature. Indeed, when the polished brass tap was turned at the front of the range, the water sputtered out in steamy spurts.

She carried the bucket to the stone sink and emptied it. At the kitchen range she placed it under the tap and straightened her back while it filled. Then she got a jug of cold water to bring it to a temperature tolerable to her raw hands and placed it on the floor. She smiled to herself as she saw Huw still playing. He was chattering away and swirling the little wooden train around on the linoleum.

The steaming water had reached a manageable level. Huw decided his little train would run onto the inviting expanse of the tiled floor. Intent on this he toddled along pulling it behind him.

She leaned forward and turned off the tap. Holding the handle with both hands she lifted the bucket, taking care to prevent the steaming water slopping over just as she had done many times before. Slowly she shuffled around and moved forward, one awkward step at a time, to set it down in the middle of the floor.

Years later, ceaselessly looking back, she could never recall the instant when she stumbled over Huw. The instant at which there was no return. The instant at which she should have seen him. She would gladly have given her whole life to reverse time and turn back the clock just for that one second. Recovering her balance, letting go of the handle, and clasping the bottom would leap into her mind at odd moments without warning. But to no avail. The bucket continued to move forward under its own momentum. Even then it wasn't inevitable. Why didn't she throw it from herself? Who would've cared about the mess? Who would've cared if the bucket had cracked a tile? Why had she not done that? Instead, instinctively, she continued to hold on to it as the near boiling water emptied over the little boy. She remembered the bucket feeling so light but she could never bring to mind what happened to it afterwards.

For the briefest moment there was a stillness, pregnant with dread. Had the water missed him? Had it poured harmlessly onto the floor? But of course not. The scream that broke the silence bore horrifying witness to that.

Until her death, it would tear into her dreams, so she would dread sleep. Sometimes in her waking moments during the day, if caught unawares, she's running with the hot trembling little bundle clutching one tiny shoe and feeling she must get to the hospital. It's just along the road, not far. She must get him there quickly, just one more road to cross. She's dodging the cars. She's panting. There's the hospital. He's quiet now. She feels his little body trembling, his breath coming in sucking gasps.

An image of her dashing into the main reception hall invades her mind. There are nurses taking him. She doesn't want to let him go. Just let me hold him. He's gone they say. But he isn't. He's there. She's still holding him. She can feel the gentle weight of him. They want to take him away but she won't let go. They bring Owain from work. 'Let me have him,' he's saying, 'just for a moment. Then we'll take him home.' But she won't let go.

Chapter Three

A village in North Wales, 2018

Miss Lottie Williams-Parry had an appointment. She was sheltering from the chill of a June south-westerly coming off the mountain. Peering through the Gothic window of the dilapidated cemetery lodge, she waited.

When the post of part-time Cemetery Liaison Officer for the village community council was offered to Miss Lottie Williams-Parry, she'd taken it on with some reluctance. *After all*, she thought, *I'm already a part-time librarian*. It was a small branch library in the village. Communicating with people seeking to locate the graves of relatives and ancestors was not what she would have seen as her métier. *Oh no, indeed, it wouldn't be me, but it isn't demanding and being an executive officer on the council is the best way of keeping my name in the public mind, the public that matters*. And it supplemented her small salary.

She had been known throughout the village as a voice coach and pianoforte teacher of the highest standard. Some years before, many years before if she was honest with herself, she was a coloratura celebrated throughout Denbighshire and renowned for her rendition of *The Queen of the Night*. In those days, no concert could be planned without her and any programme not carrying her name was considered incomplete. It was said, one year in her younger days she'd gained the stage at the National Eisteddfod, though no one could actually recall it first-hand.

He wasn't the first visitor she'd had recently. When the first one arrived at the lodge, appearing in the doorway as a dark shape with the sun behind him, he'd given her quite a start. 'It's all right to talk', he'd said. He'd cleared it with the Cemeteries Superintendent. Introducing himself, he showed his warrant and badge in a heavy-looking black leather wallet with a crest embossed in silver. How had he put it? Arrangements had been made for her to be at the disposal of a ministry in London if she agreed. Of course, if she did, she would have to sign the Official Secrets Act.

He wasn't free to say which ministry, except it was a matter of considerable significance and national security that required her assistance. She still felt a glow of self-importance and not a little excitement whenever she recalled the words he'd used. 'There is no one else in the village of sufficient social stature who could be entrusted with the task.' And she would be remunerated on a part-time basis, he said. All she had to do was pass on communications in whatever form to the address given and to send a report of anything out of the ordinary in respect of visitors to the village. She would receive instructions from time to time and, if she felt it necessary, she should contact the number he gave her immediately. She was invited to put her signature on a form which, surprisingly, already contained all her details and her address. Then he handed her a small wallet. On one leaf there was a box number address, a phone number, her identification, her photograph and a personal number. There were also words to the effect that she was not required to communicate with uniformed police officers nor them with her. The facing leaf was embossed with a silver cypher and a series of numbers and letters.

She saw her second visitor struggling with the cemetery side-gate as it reluctantly granted him access. Brushing a cobweb from the sleeve of her dark suit and smoothing the skirt, she glanced at her watch, gathered up her clipboard and handbag, and stepped out of the door.

As luck would have it, Miss Lottie Williams-Parry was well chosen, for she possessed a native curiosity bordering on impertinence. Coming towards her, she observed a man of medium height in his mid-fifties. He was of a rather stocky build with a slight limp and a full head of hair. His overcoat, worn over a suit, looked expensive. She noted he was about to take a sip from a small bottle of something but, when he spotted her, he slipped it back into his coat pocket.

At the gate, her visitor had paused to look over the cemetery falling steeply to The Nant below, as long-dormant feelings of familiarity stirred within him. For a fleeting moment he forgot the last few years, what he had experienced, and what he had done. With the clarity of vision brought through the lens of the past, he saw for the first time that the placing of the heaving mounds had been an attempt to marshal the graves in some sort of order. Nevertheless it had been defeated by rank nettles and sparse tufts of moorland grass. The view was stark and not at all like the picture carried in his mind's eye for all those years since childhood. There was the occasional crooked column or cracked sarcophagus but, in the main, there were kerbs and lichen-encrusted gravestones. Their inscriptions marked the tide of nonconformism that had engulfed the villagers in the last two centuries. *A religious movement leaving these people high and dry*, he thought. The chapels no longer the houses of God but antique emporiums, Poundlands and Wetherspoons.

In the field at the side of the cemetery stocky black cattle stood unmoving as if stilled in the act of grazing. From the west he heard the clamour of the rooks colonising a sparse coppice of birch trees. He glanced toward it highlighted as it was by the sun struggling through thin pale cloud. In the instant he turned back, the cattle had moved to a different part of the field still standing immobile as if, it seemed to him, there had been a crimp in time. The mountain loured over the cemetery as it had always done. A keen wind from the southwest brought him a brackish scent off the moors and a shiver down his spine.

Miss Lottie Williams-Parry thrust out her hand in greeting. '*Bore da*, Mr Cecil.' She pronounced his name Syssel, in the local way. 'The gentleman who emailed me, isn't it?'

He nodded. '*Bore da.*' It was a plump dimpled hand which he felt inclined to squeeze rather than shake. Even so she had a strong grip that surprised him.

8

'Miss Lottie Williams-Parry *ydw i*,' she announced. '*Sut mae?*'

So the conversation will slip in and out of Welsh, he thought. Well, perhaps it'll ease things, help matters along. '*Sut mae*. The cemetery Liaison Officer?'

'Indeed I am. I've located the plot.' She pointed with her clipboard. 'This is the way.'

She led him down a steep drive of crumbling tarmac. One of the side-paths seemed familiar to him. Somewhere along here is their grave, he recalled. Nain and Taid, Mary and Owain. *I couldn't get to Taid's funeral but I was there for Nain's. And the priest – only too glad he was to get the business over with. Who could blame him with the bitter wind coming off the mountain, whipping around his cassock?*

He became conscious of Miss Lottie Williams-Parry gently humming a tune to herself as she walked ahead of him. He found it irritating. She paused to consult her clipboard. Turning, she led him off the drive onto a narrow track running along the kerbed graves visible in the ferns and coarse weeds. 'You have to mind how you go along here, it's uneven you know.' He grunted a response. The pain in his knee had made him aware of that. They took cautious steps until she stopped abruptly. 'Well, this is the one.'

She indicated the grave plot with a gesture of the clipboard. Perched on the kerb was a rook. It broke off from grooming silky black wing feathers with its grey bill. Watchful eyes set in the purple-sheened head contemplated them, unsure on whom to focus its gaze.

Miss Lottie Williams-Parry fluttered the clipboard half-heartedly at it shouting, '*I ffwrdd bran!* Away, rook!' Reluctantly, it took to the air with a spiteful, 'kaah!'

She stepped onto the gravelled top of the grave and using the clipboard she began to flatten the rough grass so that she could read the inscription. Cecil felt a flash of irritation. This was an intrusion. The woman should go away now. She started to recite the faded inscription on the lichened kerb. He heard his own name, 'Huw Syssel.' The skin on the back of his neck tightened as if cold water was being poured on it. The grave swam before his eyes and for a moment he must have tottered, prompting her to ask, 'Are you alright Mr Syssel?'

9

He nodded and she went on, 'dear child of Owain and Mary Syssel of 9 Railway Terrace, Llangollen. Died on the twenty-second of February, nineteen fifty-six, aged three years.'

She glanced up at him, 'Well, that's it. I'll be leaving you now, Mr Syssel, yes?'

'Huw Cecil,' he snapped. He was not sure of his feelings nor why he spoke out so meanly, expressing them with the brittle edge of his words as he did. Then he softened his voice a little, '*formerly* of 9 Railway Terrace, Llangollen.'

Chapter Four

For an instant, her face was without expression. Unblinking, her eyes held his as bewilderment and confusion played on her features in turn. Her gaze flicked over the clipboard and down to the grave before falling on him again. Quizzically, she said, 'Owain and Mary – they were from the village here?'

He gave a curt nod.

'But they weren't your parents, were they?'

Like him, she was struggling with the facts and he found her questions intrusive. He was wishing he'd not let himself be drawn into this kind of exchange.

'I mean, that's not you there, is it?' she went on.

'They're my grandparents. They're buried over on the other side.' He pointed up the path. 'They were from the village. Both born here.'

'That's it. Your grandparents. And living in the same house you were from, is it, in Llangollen?'

He felt obliged to answer. 'They moved to the house next door. It must have been soon after . . .' he nodded to the grave, 'it happened, I suppose. I grew up in number nine. My parents took it when it became empty.'

'Oh, I see, and you were named for him. That poor little boy. Bit of a responsibility for you that.'

He heard himself ask sharply, 'What do you mean?'

'What do I mean?' She paused a moment a little taken aback. 'Well, you having to go on with his life wasn't it? Live it for him, like.'

11

Impulsively, he cast off the line of their dialogue. 'Thank you for your help this morning, Miss Williams-Parry. *Hwyl fawr.*'

'Yes of course. Well, I'll leave you to it now, Mr Syssel. *Hwyl fawr.*' She placed her clipboard under her arm and started to retrace her steps along the path. Pausing for a moment she turned as if she was going to speak but then continued along the path.

He took out one of his phones, his personal one, and focused it on the lettering of the kerb. As he took some images, he could see her walking up the driveway unwrapping a mint she'd taken out of her handbag. Reaching the main gates she popped it in her chubby mouth before casting a furtive glance over her shoulder so their eyes met over the phone. Giving a shrug and a toss of her loose red hair she turned away.

Seeing the grave for the first time since learning of its existence, the questions came to him. *Why was I so named after a life cut short just three years before my own birth? A little boy who would've been my uncle; and why did all the family choose, indeed must have connived, to keep it from me?* He had to fit the deeply embedded fragments of memory together to provide the hidden story. Then he knew he would have to face up to the completed picture.

Fumbling for cigarettes in his coat pocket he remembered he'd given up the smoking years ago. *Strange how I've forgotten. As though the visit to the grave has thrown me back in time.* Looking up at the wind-driven overcast he saw the rook was still loitering overhead, waiting to get its perch back. *What's so special about this place, bran? What do you know about it?*

Why he was conscious of being observed, he wouldn't have been able to explain. It was something experience had brought him over time. Perhaps it was some movement at the margin of his vision.

Chapter Five

He turned his eyes in the direction of the gate without moving his head. It was a mechanical act, born of training and practice. There was nothing to be seen, but *something* had triggered his senses. Was it a man, perhaps more than one? If it was going to be a hit, it would have been done at the graveside . . . unless – unless that cemetery woman had been in the way. *Shit! I've made a mistake leaving myself wide open.*

There was the familiar tingling in the spine. Crouching and ignoring the stab of pain in his knee he moved swiftly to put a gravestone between himself and the gate. Sliding his hand under his jacket he eased the 9 millimetre Glock 17 automatic pistol in its underarm holster. The watchers would still be around somewhere, observing or waiting for their chance.

He left the cemetery the way he had come, feeling unsettled and tense. The village seemed unreal and illusory as if he was floating dreamlike down the street.

It must be fifty years or more since I came through the cemetery holding Nain's hand, he thought. *A regular weekly ritual after catching the bus in Llangollen for the short ride to the village. First we would go round the shops, Watkins Hardware for matches, scouring pads and such. And perhaps Aaron Tudor Drapers for cotton, tape or wool. Always we would call at Hughes the cake shop for a tiny boat-shaped confection with a marzipan sail. Then we'd sit in the park looking over to the mountain while I ate it, the sail first. Then we would set off to the reading room of the small public library for Nain to browse the pages of the village newspaper,* Y Gloch. *Finally we'd follow the top path*

*of the cemetery as she pointed down the slope to show me the graves of relatives.
She would always recite who they were and where they were from but she never
mentioned the grave I saw today or that the little boy had ever existed. The little
boy who died three years before I was born. Why?* The question flared up
in his mind.

Cecil turned onto the high street where he'd left his car at the
kerb. It was the only one in sight, a nondescript grey Honda Civic.
The number plate showed it to be twelve years old, although the
other pair of plates in the boot indicated only ten years. The street
seemed as empty to him as it would have been on those bowler-
hatted Sundays of his childhood in the late fifties of the last century.
Then, not even a dog would dare to sully the Sabbath by appearing
on it. Down the hill in the far distance to the east, was the Cheshire
plain and, beyond it, the sharply lit Peckforton hills, foretelling rain.
A once-familiar sight.

In a flash, he realised he was letting his guard slip. The vulnerability of his position triggered his training and experience. For the
benefit of the watcher, he walked past the car, as if on impulse. He
recalled the coffee bar that used to be on the corner of the next junction: Marinetti's. It looked jaded now but its plate glass window was
still sweeping around the corner in a dynamic curve, bringing the
look of the thirties to the village decades ago. He decided to go in
and position himself so he could see up the street. Whoever was at
the cemetery would have to come into the open and follow him
down toward the corner either to make the hit or leave altogether.
There would be no point in going the other way over the moors to
the west.

Looking in through the window, the high stools were empty. A
pair of tall chromium urns gently steamed on a shelf against the far
wall. A man stood behind the bar in a white shirt, black bow tie, and
soda jerk's side cap. It conveyed a boyish look to his face. But it gave
the lie to his age, as his arthritic hands wiping the metal top revealed.
A card hung on the door bearing the words *ar agor*, meaning open.
Open. He pushed at the full-length glass panel and stepped in. The
bar curved to follow the contour of the window and an end stool

offered an unhindered view up and down the street. It presented a clear field of fire. If necessary it would give him the first shot.

Should I switch my iPhone on? he thought.

This was no ordinary iPhone, not since Tech-Ops downloaded a file from a disguised website when they issued it to him as standard for operatives in the field. It told Control of his precise position as he was moving and the speed at which he was travelling, even when it was switched off. When it was on, they could monitor all that he said. Emails sent from it went first to a Germany-based domain. The address was a front that automatically encrypted them and simultaneously forwarded them through a circuitous route of servers to Thames House and Vauxhall Cross. Then on to Guy Hackett, his controller in command of the operation in North Wales. *Better leave it off, keep this to myself as long as possible.* He'd been ordered to maintain radio silence anyway. As it was, they would want to know what he was doing in the cemetery in the first place or even in the village. Something he'd have to explain later, or perhaps not at all.

They can take it or leave it. He hadn't wanted to be reinstated all these years after his implausible retirement in 2001. Retirement due to, how was it put to him, 'a conflict of interest, making his position incompatible with the aims of the Service'. After that, they kept him on a lead all the time, suggesting he'd need to keep a firearm for self-protection, he recalled. The three-monthly range practice, sessions at the police driving school in the Midlands, and regular health checks went along with it as mandatory. They'd yanked him back with the so-called invitation to accept reinstatement. An invitation he couldn't refuse if he wanted to stay alive, they'd implied. For if he declined, he would lose his weapon status and any information and protection to which he was entitled. And he *did* need that protection, they stressed. Without so much as a by-your-leave, they told him he was reassigned to Thames House. They needed someone in the field in North Wales for about two to three months, they said. He was issued with a current up-rated weapon and ammunition. He also received a self-administering field kit in the form of a fentanyl lollipop blister pack attached to the inside of his jacket. It was an

15

improvement on the ampoule needle familiar to him, they said. He was also reissued with a warrant and a false identity, including a wallet of bank cards with activated accounts. He also had another phone of which he was pretty certain they had no knowledge. Nor did they know he had taken advantage of the situation to organise his visit to the cemetery, or he hoped they didn't. He'd felt a compulsion to visit that grave.

They wanted an old Moscow and Berlin hand who knew how things fitted together back then. There was no one to match his years of experience and expertise in bringing operators over from the other side in the chaos of those times, they said. That one in particular, Voronov; well, what other choice existed especially as Cecil himself had grown up in the area? Besides, cuts in the overall budget made him a cheap option.

Voronov: the name raised feelings he thought he had buried. The time in Berlin: he still had the flashbacks, but only occasionally now. The tablets helped but not as much as the scotch. They'd tried to convince him this time they were going to do the honourable thing with the material Voronov had. He'd allowed them to think they'd succeeded. He didn't believe they would. No, not for one minute. Now the question was what would they do with *him* when they got it, knowing what was in it as he did?

A large mug of black coffee and an encrusted sugar shaker were set down before him on the tacky counter.

'I didn't say I wanted this.' He was irritated at this interruption to his chain of thought.

'What do you mean?' The virtual soda jerk looked puzzled.

He asked tartly, 'Suppose I wanted the ice cream soda you're dressed to serve?'

The man glanced down at his outfit. 'Well, too bad! There's nothing else here. This is a coffee bar an' that's coffee, like.'

'Not even tea?'

He shrugged. 'Not even tea.' He placed a handful of milk capsules on the counter and disappeared through a door at the side of the urns.

Cecil felt a faint tinge of remorse at his mean observation. Ignoring the capsules, he took a cautious sip of the coffee, careful not to skin his mouth as he felt the heat of the liquid on his face. He winced at the bitter taste and, taking the bottle from his pocket, he measured a capful of amber liquid into the mug. From outside, the feeble clink-clink of a bell, a familiar light sound, infiltrated the steamy interior reawakening patterns in his mind. They triggered a flash of recollection. *Of course, it comes from St. Tydfil's next to the cemetery.* It timidly marked the hour twelve times.

Ah, the cemetery, he reflected. *When I saw the grave this morning it was more moving, more forceful, than coming upon the stuff a month before while I sorted through those things in that old shoebox of Mam's.* She, Gwyneth, had died at the turn of the year.

There was the black-edged funeral card, the two scrappy photographs, and the flimsy yellowed cuttings from the local paper. One reporting on the tragic accident and the other giving an account of the funeral. *They must have come into Mam's possession after Nain died.*

What was it the woman in the cemetery said: I'd had to go on with this little boy's life? Is that indeed what I've done? The question waylaid him again as it had since he found out about his namesake. The photographs fell from his fingers fluttering onto the table. Would this boy have gone to the same school? Quite possibly. Would he have had the same career? Something stirred in his mind as he realised in the eyes of the rest of his family he was living a life for the little boy.

Military service in the Intelligence Corps, basic training at Pirbright, a corporal after twenty-nine weeks. Six months later posted to officer training. Second lieutenant within a year. Then training in languages and after that the Berlin posting. Followed by reading Modern Languages at Oxford. Recruitment into the Service by his tutor in the last term of his final year. He recalled how it was put, 'Shall we talk about your prospects?' Even so, his career that followed, his marriage, his life, all his actions and decisions were probably determined by the reason for his coming into existence. *And did I meet the expectations of Nain, Taid and Dad, filling out their image of the dead little boy? How have I measured up to them? So was that it? Has the purpose of my life been a child's resurrection? Nothing more than a substitute born in the shadow of another? Good God*, he realised, *I wouldn't be here if it weren't for that little boy's death.*

In his mind he had to seize back the person he thought he was and endure this assault on his self. After his discovery, the Service had contacted him out of the blue and explained what they wanted him for. Thus a glimmer of an opportunity was kindled, an opportunity to deal with his identity dilemma and become his own man again. This time to impose his will on the situation and not the collective will of some agency. When they explained his posting up to North Wales, he decided to seek out the grave. As the moment of reflection waned he picked up the photographs and put them back in his wallet.

Suddenly his senses were alerted. Up the street, on the opposite side, a male in a woollen cap pulled down over his ears was walking purposefully as if he was on his way somewhere. He felt the familiar tingling tautening his nerves and steadying him. A single bead of sweat trickled down his spine like a cold insect. The man seemed to be going anywhere but the coffee bar, his shoulders hunched against the wind, his hands thrust into a dark windcheater. He gave a quick look backwards. That was the give-away, a preparatory glance, revealing he knew where his target was. If he was up for it, he'd take a shot from across the street as he drew level. Cecil eased the Glock out of its holster, chambered a round, and slipped the safety.

When he thought back, he would recall a feeling of heightened awareness. Each action occurring in a series of freeze-frame moments of intensity. There were scenes flashing at intervals, as if time had slowed. Aim, take up first pressure on the trigger, and squeeze. The shot was deafening within the constrained space. The curved plate glass, shattering into shards, seemed to descend like sheets of ice before turning into a slow-motion blizzard of slivers bursting out onto the street. Life seems to stand still when a gun fires and things are changed forever.

In the following stillness, he went over to the wrecked window. There was gun smoke in the air and the familiar smell of cordite as he stepped out, conscious of the glass crunching underfoot. All the

18

time, he kept the figure covered. It was on its side, slumped against the wall. He'd always thought it strange how a dead body looked less of a person than it does in life a moment before. How entirely changed the human form is by the absence of life. The woollen hat was still on a head lying on its left arm as if at rest, but the body bore no resemblance to a sleeping form. The soft-nosed bullet had done its work well, leaving a thin dark trickle from a small puckered hole on the forehead just over the right eye. The lid was half-closed as if stilled in the act of winking. The wall behind was splattered with a grey putty-like substance speckled with blood and fragments of bone. Tufts of hair on pieces of scalp amid strands of wool were smeared on the masonry. On the ground, blood was pooling and already thickening. The right hand still clutched a heavy-calibre pistol.

Miss Lottie Williams-Parry caught his eye, scurrying down the street as she kept glancing back over her ample quivering shoulder, her phone pressed urgently to her ear. That was why he missed the male figure stealing out of a shop doorway and following her eventually to her house. Cecil assumed she was calling the police, wrongly, as it turned out. The pseudo soda jerk was standing bare-headed in front of the urns, his eyes staring fixedly ahead. Coffee had slopped down the front of his white shirt. His hands were gripping the bar top and his whole body trembled. He would stay like this until half an hour later when a police officer would prise his fingers open one by one.

Chapter Six

Huw Cecil had always felt Llangollen on the river Dee, the town where he was born and grew up, was a place with history. Dinas Bran, a ruined castle once a stronghold of the princes of Powys, occupied a prominent hilltop above a township dominated by a great limestone outcrop known as the Eglwyseg Escarpment.

The ground floors of an Edwardian terrace of shiny red brick on Castle Street are given over to small shops and cafés. The floors above are mostly occupied with dingy flats. Cecil had been standing in the window of a pub opposite for twenty minutes watching a discreet red pinprick of light flashing in the window of a particular top floor flat. It indicated he'd been followed. Then it changed to green. The coast was clear. Grabbing his overcoat and downing his double scotch, he went over to the bar and placed the empty glass on it. As he turned to go he felt a hand on his bottom. It gave a gentle squeeze. A woman sitting on a bar stool next to him leaned over and murmured in his ear, 'Do you feel like another one, *cariad*?'

Taken aback, he turned to her. She was someone who might have been pretty once but whose attractions were long washed out. Thrown off balance, he shook his head coyly.

'Oh well, never mind. But it's nice to be fancied, isn't it?'

A little disturbed, he left the pub and crossed the street. Still flustered, he cursed when the key – he'd picked it up at the drop-box back in Green Park – stuck as he turned it in the lock of the shabby door beside the cake shop. It opened on the second attempt. The stairwell was lit by the door's grimy fanlight and a wired skylight at the top of the building. A single unlit bulb hung by a length of flex furry with dust. He stepped around a bicycle propped against the shiny dark-brown wall and ascended the stairs, conscious of his footsteps sounding on the bare treads and the burn in his knee. Loud pop music came from a door on the first floor. The smell of bacon and cooking fat pervaded the fusty air, making him light-headed as he tried not to breathe. Stepping around a soggy cardboard box of empties, he went on up. Shouting came from behind one of the doors on the landing of the second floor. It was wrenched open confronting him with a jowly young man in a vest revealing a spider web tattoo on his neck. He stopped abruptly and Cecil felt his eyes following him as he climbed to the top floor. He found the door he was looking for and gave a single light tap on the panel. Almost immediately he heard the chains being unlatched.

Two men appeared at the door. He assumed they were Hackett's lieutenants. They led him through into the main room.

'Mr Cecil, sir.' The shorter, more muscular one, looking ex-military, acknowledged him respectfully. 'Just one round discharged was there, sir?' He held out his hand for the weapon. Cecil nodded and handed it over, looking around the room.

There were two shabby armchairs facing each other across a sticky coffee table. Guy Hackett, Cecil's controller, was sitting in one, his back to a tiled fireplace with an electric heater. It looked as if it hadn't been switched on since the nineteen-fifties. At the rear of the room were a Formica-topped table and two kitchen chairs, a shelf holding an electric kettle, unwashed mugs, tea bags, sugar, powdered milk, and a sink with a single dripping tap. The window, the one with the warning light, looked over the street through yellowing net. In the corner, the radio frequency detection and communications equipment was quietly buzzing and looking incongruous in the squalid room. The air was chill and damp. He decided to keep his coat on.

'So,' Hackett leaned forward in his chair, 'either they followed you to the village or they were waiting for you, two of them. One of them must have held back as an observer and back up. Obviously he was too far off to be of any immediate use, luckily for you, but he sent a report. GCHQ picked it up, decrypted it and sent it on to the Office. They sent it on to me. He will arrive any time now hot on your heels.' There was a pause as he let the information sink in. 'It seems you've conveniently led them here,' he snapped. 'That's why we held you back on a red. Within five hours he's being joined by at least one other. We think they may set up a control station here.'

Cecil made no response. This was not a good start to their first meeting.

Guy Hackett had been born in the Home Counties. After King's School Canterbury he went from Cambridge, where he failed to take his degree, to a job in Whitehall, put forward and vouched for by an uncle in the Foreign Office. After posts in several foreign embassies, being only too pleased to move him on, he was approached by MI5. Probably thanks to another uncle in the Foreign Office. This led to his recruitment. He embraced his duties with unbridled fervour driven by ambition, perhaps, to prove to himself and to his family that he could achieve without help from them. But then there was "the incident". Things did not go well at the internal inquiry. It all landed on his desk. This assignment was his last chance.

He gestured impatiently to the other chair. 'Oh, do sit down, Cecil. This is Lessing. He's on detachment from Tech-Ops.' He nodded to the tall angular man who was about to join his companion sitting at the table. 'And you've met Kerr. He's just joined us. Weapons are one of his virtues.'

Hackett paused and leaned back before speaking. 'That was quite a stir you caused. It seems there's been nothing like it in the village since a murder in 1947. We've moved swiftly but we failed to keep it away from the police, you see. The local uniforms are clearing things up, under our supervision, of course. They're taking the stance that they've a description of the gunman and they're searching for him in the Liverpool area. The media have been informed it was a drugs-related incident. The police counselling unit are dealing with the coffee bar man and we're having the damaged window repaired quickly. So hopefully it'll be a seven-day wonder in the local papers. Apparently there's only one company in this part of the world that deals with curved glass.'

As he gingerly lowered himself into the armchair with the lightest of contact with his hands Cecil noticed Hackett had been picking absently at the tattered fabric of his chair with his long thin fingers. There were clean unravelled strands lying along the greasy arm.

'I expect you'd like to know who they're working for, unless you've already figured it out?'

Of course Cecil had figured it out. He felt a rush of irritation by what he thought was Hackett's affected frivolousness. In an exaggerated manner he queried, 'Would it be the SVR by any chance?'

'Yes. Your old friends from the nineties.' If he'd noticed Cecil's equally affected nonchalance, Hackett didn't reveal it. They both knew the SVR was an agency for intelligence and espionage activities outside the Russian Federation, the equivalent of MI6, working from its headquarters at Yasenevo, near Moscow. In foreign affairs it has authority over the FSB, the Foreign Intelligence Agency of the Russian Federation, and the successor to the KGB with its Moscow headquarters at Lubyanka Square.

A tractor roared through the bottleneck of manure spattered four-by-fours down on the street, setting the sash window frames rattling. Hackett paused for the noise to subside, his bald head catching the pale light from the window. 'How are you feeling after the incident? Steady, no backlash? Rather a close brush I'd say.' He waited for an answer.

Cecil gave a cool almost imperceptible shake of his head.

'You did have a nasty experience in Berlin so I'm told,' Hackett persisted. 'It seems it left you with quite a bit of aftershock, possibly having some bearing on the rather contradictory stance leading to the premature termination of your career. Or so the record says anyway.' he added dismissively.

Cecil saw a faint chance of escape. 'Yes, well, if that's the way you see it, why not let me go? It's not too late.'

Hackett fixed him with a stare. It accentuated the almost hypnotic blue eyes with which nature had endowed him. They were further emphasised by his wire-framed spectacles. Taking a handkerchief out of the top pocket of his jacket he made to take them off but in an odd gesture he changed his mind, stuffing it back. Then he moved his stare slightly to the side. The effect was offset by the incipient tic in his left eye. In a hushed but incisive voice, a voice that could rise from a rasp to a scream, he said, 'You know as well as I do this is not going to happen.' He paused. 'So, leaving aside for the time being the question as to why you went off-piste and switched off your phone – oh and by the way, old boy, you have us intrigued as to why you should visit a cemetery,' Hackett paused again lifting his voice slightly as he returned to the main question, 'how the hell did they know where you were going?'

Cecil settled himself and clasped his hands to control them, becoming aware of the small mound of his stomach. He could still smell the frying bacon fat mingling with an overall air of dampness and stale tobacco. For some moments it would have looked to the unfamiliar as if he wasn't going to answer and he noticed, with some satisfaction, Hackett's uneasy glance toward Lessing. Cecil raised his head to contemplate him and Kerr at the table. Kerr had an aluminium case open before him while he removed the magazine from the Glock, cleaned the weapon and replaced the used round with surprising dexterity for someone with such big-knuckled hands. They seemed able to crush a man's larynx with no effort at all. Lessing was looking on, coolly smoking, his oval protruding eyes fixed on the gun. The poor light in the room emphasised the hollows beneath his high cheek bones and his pointed chin. Kerr latched the magazine into the pistol-butt and pressed it home with two clicks. A truck ground up to the traffic lights at the junction with the A5, its brakes coming on with a prolonged hiss. Cecil allowed a few moments of tension before he turned to Hackett and eased himself in his chair. 'No one could have known beforehand where I was going, no one except—'

'Except the cemetery liaison woman. Yes, we know,' Hackett broke in.

'You do?' Cecil was surprised. The initiative was taken from him.

24

'She's clean. We checked her when we set her up some time ago. She's been keeping an eye on you since you emailed her to make that cemetery appointment before you came up. She saw what happened today. It was she who alerted us. It seems she followed you. She did quite well actually, except her address is compromised. The other man followed her home. He included it in his report to the opposition. We've given her a full assessment. She's got the potential to develop and, though she doesn't know it yet, we're thinking of taking her on as a full-time asset, training her up and so on.'

Peeved, Cecil asked, 'How many more assets have you set up without telling me?'

'We covered the zone of interest around Llangollen as soon as we knew Voronov headed up this way to hole up.' Hackett shrugged. 'Normal routine – you know that. By the way, old boy, your house at Hammersmith must have been watched and you didn't spot it. That's not like the Huw Cecil I hear about.' Hackett's eyes narrowed briefly, boring into his. 'Preoccupied with something, old boy?'

Cecil said nothing returning Hackett's gaze. The tension was palpable as he left him waiting for an answer.

Irritated by his silence, Hackett thrust his head forward. 'They couldn't have known where you were going, except you were on your way, so they put a tail on you and you put them off the scent leading him to that cemetery. Unwittingly, it turned out, so you get no credit for it, as it could have gone terribly wrong. Clearly they intended to take you out of the game once you'd led them to Voronov's whereabouts. We can assume they thought he was somewhere in that village. But not anymore. That's why we're moving house before they come into town. We're not going far, just on the border.' He leaned back. 'You've changed your number plates round?'

'Yes, of course.' Cecil felt a stab of annoyance. He still had a painful nick on his thumb from one of the clips to remind him.

With a mental start, the question arose overwhelming him: was Hackett right? He became conscious of the weight of his discovery of his namesake challenging his sense of self. And how it had borne down on him, dominating his thoughts, so he'd let things slip. Perhaps the whole business was getting out of hand. What had gone wrong in Hammersmith? He looked back, charting his movements.

I started the car outside the house at Mall Road and never left it until I got out at the village except the stop at the service station. Even so, it looks as if I've been followed all the way in relays. How did I miss the watch on the house? Nothing significant on the CCTV, the usual callers, the same postman who'd been cleared, and the same team of refuse men. They were all cleared, no callers, electricity, gas, the usual passers-by, except – except that woman with the guide dog, a beautiful black Labrador. She'd been passing the house each morning for the past two or three weeks. He often saw her late afternoons as well, going the same way. *Shit. How had I let that go?* He sensed his stomach sinking with shame and humiliation, seeing himself as others may be seeing him: a worn-out spy, yesterday's man. In a flash, his feelings turned to cold anger. He had only himself to blame.

Hackett broke into his thinking. 'You've worked on him before, old boy, in Berlin when you tried to bring him over from the SVR. What do you think he's up to and why the hell did he hold on to that stuff at the time, if it was so hot?'

'I think I know why but, right now, you think he's somewhere in this area, perhaps in this town, waiting for a chance to come over?'

Hackett nodded.

'You've enquired around, I assume; hotel rooms and such?'

'Not yet. We don't want to alert him.'

'Well, he doesn't trust you, that's clear. As for me, I wish he did, for I wouldn't be here, but his lack of trust is not surprising. We left him out on a limb, Berlin '99, I remember. We threw him to the wolves.' Cecil paused, his anger still smouldering, though now he transferred it to Hackett. He said, 'If I remember rightly, you were only a senior operative before the move to Thames House. Babcock House in Gower Street, wasn't it? On attachment to the Home Office?' He paused. 'Yes, I recall it now. After the "unfortunate business" that led to the inquiry.'

Hackett ignored his barbs. 'According to the record, it was you who left him out on a limb. You walked out on him and the Service.'

Disregarding the smart aroused by the riposte, Cecil said, 'Speaking about the record, the other side must have found out as much about me as you have when they reopened Voronov's file, and mine, I expect. But how do they know I've been brought back?'

Hackett leaned forward. 'Unknown to him, the SVR operatives followed Lev Voronov to the UK via the Russian embassy. We didn't know what he was up to at that stage in the game so, after a token investigation, we let him in and tailed the operatives as well as him.'

'You used him as bait.'

'Quite.'

'How did he contact the Service?'

'He used a call box for the initial contact so his mobile couldn't be traced. He gave us time to get ourselves together, calling back from another box within the time he set. Unfortunately for him, he was followed on both occasions. Our tail reported the SVR operatives playing a laser mic on the kiosk window so they must've picked up both sides of the calls. Your name was mentioned when he asked for you, as a condition of the transaction involving some material he claimed to possess. When we opened your file we found out it was the stuff from the Lubyanka that went wild sometime in the nineties.'

'That would be the material you told me about when you contacted me. The stuff from the Berlin Friendship House we went after before?'

'Yes. As you know, all on microfilm before the KGB destroyed the original files. There were videos, still photos, audio tapes, the whole lot. We can also assume the SVR deduced you were back in the game though they didn't know the extent to which you've been kept on ice, so to speak. But by now, after the business in the village, well . . .'

'And the material itself, where is it now?'

'It's either still in London or he's stashed it here somewhere. He's unlikely to be carrying it around with him. He told us he brought ten rolls out of Russia, still on the original microfilm.'

'Do you think he's copied it?'

'Unlikely. There's a lot of it and I don't see how he has access to the necessary equipment. He could get a private firm to do it for him I suppose. Just in case, we'll take measures after we get it.'

Cecil looked at him hard. '*Measures*?'

'Yes. You know.' Hackett paused uncomfortably.

'And you've offered him the usual, I suppose; citizenship, money – security?'

'Of course.'

'Of course,' Cecil echoed. There was a long pause as he looked hard at Hackett. 'And then?'

Hackett affected puzzlement. 'And then – what, old boy?'

'And you'll pass it on to the proper authorities for them to act on it?'

'Of course, old boy. Look, we've been through all this at the outset. It seems to me you're still thinking they'll suppress the material as they intended last time.'

'As you would have intended last time if you had been in the position you are now.'

'Well the wind is blowing from a different direction now and I blow with it. These are different times. I thought we'd convinced you – put your mind at rest.'

Cecil was finding it difficult to suppress his rising irritation. 'Then why interfere? Let the other side extract the material from Voronov and reveal the whole thing. The UK public prosecutor asks for the evidence and acts on it.'

Hackett paused briefly, his mouth hardening. 'I must say your pretention of naiveté is *almost* convincing, old boy.' He turned to Kerr. 'What do you think of his acting?'

Kerr smiled obligingly. 'He's very good isn't he, sir?'

Turning back, Hackett's tone became icy. 'Now look here, Cecil, you no more believe they would release it into the hands of the UK authorities in the interests of justice than I do. They'll exploit the whole package and take any opportunity for blackmail before threatening to use it to destabilise the foundations of western regimes unless – well, you know.'

'Unless what?'

'Unless the Russian Federation is left free to conduct its programme of territorial expansion and world domination of energy resources without hindrance. It could even lead to the complete collapse of the NATO Alliance – Putin's main aim.' Hackett leaned back as if to emphasise what he was about to say. 'Come on, Cecil, you know as well as we do why the SVR are chasing Voronov for all they're worth. It's the same reason the material was harvested by the KGB at the Berlin Friendship House in the first place. If they get to him before we do, it's all up.'

'I'm impressed by your enlightened view on what should be done with the material – *old boy*,' Cecil said. 'Are you sure it's shared by the powers that be?'

Hackett ignored the sarcasm. 'Cecil, you know what we have to do.' Leaning towards him he went on. 'All right, I grant you there'll have to be some careful selection. If it's used in the wrong way, too freely, the information on that microfilm, some of it,' he paused in exasperation, 'well it will need to be balanced against the national interest. If it gets out, it will change profoundly the way people in the West see their past and present regimes, particularly in the UK.' He took a deep breath. 'And that is all we have to be concerned about. Our role is over the minute the film is handed to the appropriate authority. It's not for us to decide what to do with it.'

'Used in the wrong way?' Cecil spat out the query. 'You mean if it is used without protecting certain individuals of the highest rank.' Surprised by a flash of anger now, he would have his say. The phrases tumbled out on top of each other, 'certain bodies – the dark forces – the real seats of power – the old establishment and vested interest set above the democratic system – holding power secretly over the nation state.'

As he spoke, he became conscious of his feelings hardening. If he got his hands on that material, he would see it was not suppressed. This was his chance to impose his own decisions, his own judgment, based on his morality, not the actions of the Service. *Do they think I'm one of them? To hand it over for, how did Hackett put it, 'careful selection' in order to protect those evil – in the national interest? The national interest lies in seeing evil is punished, surely.*

Out of the blue he became aware of the wrath turned not just on the security service he had so loyally worked for in the past, but on himself for not having the courage to go through with the business before when the material was within his grasp.

Hackett held up his hand to silence him. His eyes stared piercingly into Cecil's. Too long, apparently. The left one started twitching. Light glinted off his spectacles as he felt around in his jacket pockets for cigarettes. Not finding them, he gave up and spoke, his voice cold and calculated, 'Oh, you may have the luxury of saying and thinking what you like in this room, Cecil, but let me remind you, old boy: though you may still be held in some regard by elements at Vauxhall Cross, somewhat unwarranted in the light of current events in my view, you have no choice in your actions. You're at the disposal of MI5 to do with you however it chooses. And, if it so chooses . . .' Unhooking his spectacles he held them between the finger and thumb of one hand, looking at them thoughtfully before raising his head. 'Oh, but why am I talking like this, old boy? As if it would ever come to that.' His thin smile never quite reached his glass-hard eyes. 'Obviously we must assume they're looking for you as well as Voronov. At this stage it's up to him to make contact. Let's hope, when he makes his move, he doesn't alert them. The rest is up to you now.' He pointed his spectacles at him, 'You grew up here, didn't you? You must know this place and the surrounding area like the back of your hand.' Carefully hooking the spectacles on his ears he asked, 'When were you last here?'

Cecil shrugged. 'I can't remember. It's too long ago.'

Hackett looked at him. 'You haven't been back in over forty years, have you?'

Detecting a note of condescension in his voice, Cecil considered a fitting answer before being content with a slow nod and saying, 'It must be something like that.'

'Where was it you lived?' Hackett persisted. 'I mean, which part of the town?'

The point being made was not lost on Cecil. As far as Hackett was concerned the gulf of background between them was unbridgeable and, despite his reputation, he belonged in the same rank as Lessing and Kerr. But he wouldn't rise to it. Dismissively he said, 'It was a terrace on the other side of the river, demolished decades ago I believe.'

'Well we've arranged for you to stay at Gales. It's a small hotel and wine bar around the corner, on Bridge Street. I don't suppose it existed in your day. I believe it has a good restaurant. I'm told the cellar is well stocked. By the way, old boy, don't attempt to come back here. From tonight all trace of us will be gone. I have to go down to Birmingham for a face-to-face report. Kerr will see you out and you can hand your key to him as you go. We'll contact you about the next establishment in due course. It's just over the border, Oswestry way. I'm being given an expanded station with quite a staff. It's a reflection of the weight given to this operation. Can't tell you anything more right now, need to know basis, you know how it is. Obviously we'll be monitoring your movements and so will Millbank. Oh – and do keep your iPhone on but don't break radio silence until you are with him. We don't want any more extra-mural incidents, do we?'

As Cecil rose to leave, Kerr handed over the Glock. 'There you are. All cleaned and ready to go. Just a signature here and your key if you don't mind, sir.'

When he was at the door, Hackett called, 'Cecil!'

He turned back.

'Good luck.'

He gave a cursory nod, glanced at Lessing holding the door open, and left the room.

Hackett listened to his steps on the bare treads. At the sound of the street door closing he pointed to Kerr and gestured to the window. Moving over to it and fingering the net curtain aside, Kerr peered out. 'He's clear.'

At the same time, Lessing called from his place at the communications equipment, 'He's switched his iPhone off. He's off-air.'

31

'I thought he might do that,' Hackett said. 'Don't tail him, he's bound to spot you. You'll just have to track him, bearing in mind it's his phone you're tracking not necessarily him. The Tech-Ops people will be here soon. You can stay with them while I'm down at Birmingham and we'll all meet up later at the Oswestry place. Tell them they're to keep the equipment running during the move.'

'Are we bringing in the local unit of Special Branch sir?' Kerr asked.

'No. We're to keep this close in. Those are strict orders.' Hackett turned to Lessing. 'Do you know where his car is?'

'It's parked around the corner but he'll move it to the hotel later, I'm sure.'

Hackett pondered for a moment. 'Get them to plant a trace in it before he pootles off. That should help, in case he tries any funny business – and while you're at it, get GCHQ to put a flag on his cards. Remember he's the fly-paper. That's what we're using him for.' And in an undertone more to himself than the others, he said, 'Something he's only too aware of.'

Chapter Seven

As Cecil was on his way to check in at the hotel, a thin early evening rain had set in making the pavements gleam. He was prompted to glance up to catch a glimpse of Dinas Bran but it was blanketed in a chilling mist. Stepping in the newsagent's on the corner of Oak Street and picking up the *Daily Telegraph* he spoke to the man at the counter, 'I don't suppose you have foreign newspapers?'

'Er, no boy, we don't. No call for 'em, see.'

'I shall be staying here for a while and I was wondering whether you could order one for me. I would pick it up each day.'

'Oh, I think we could do that. Staying in the town itself, are you?'

Cecil nodded.

'And where's that then?'

'At Gales Hotel.'

'Ah yes. Nice place.' He took up a pen holding it ready at a notepad, 'And what paper shall I order?'

'*Izvestia*. The Russian version if you could get it.'

'*Izvestia*.' The newsagent looked up from his pad. 'The Russian version?'

'Yes.'

He made a note on his pad. 'And what name is it?'

'Smith.'

The newsagent lifted his head. 'Smith, is it?'

Cecil gave him a pale smile and nodded. 'Smith.'

'OK, Mr Smith they'll be coming in from the day after tomorrow.'

Cecil thanked him and stepped out of the door. *Well, that's given the tree a good shaking*, he thought. *If Voronov's anywhere around here he'll soon know where I'm staying.*

Chapter Eight

He finished his glass of wine and sat back. There was a thick stone wall behind him he'd noted and his room on the top floor looked out over a wide yard with no fire escapes on that side of the building. The street was narrow with only four paces from the door of the bar to the frontage opposite. *No cover there*, he thought. From the table in the dimly lit corner of the panelled room he listened to the gentle buzz of conversation from the few drinkers and diners, including a couple of chess players. It had been a good meal: onion soup followed by griddled polenta with a red Bordeaux, Ch. Bernadotte 2012, medium-bodied, slightly tart. *Hackett was right, they do have a good cellar here.*

He stretched his legs under the table, easing his knee. Ah, to relax for a brief spell. To let thoughts and images rise. *Why had Nain not told me?* He sat up. The question rose from the depths and burst in his mind like a star shell. *She'd all but raised me. I spent so much time in her house. Especially in those early years when Mam was working after Dad's death. The house next door was an extension of my own.* The sudden thought brought images to his mind's eye with a sharpness bordering on hallucination. There was the pendulum-stilled clock on the kitchen wall always showing quarter past ten and the religious pictures on the landing at the top of the stairs.

He is playing on the landing. Nain has just stepped out into the street to pay the coalman. There is the tall door of the cupboard he is forbidden to open. He has never been told why. Somehow it makes the ban more powerful, more mysterious and he could never reach the door handle anyway. But he is eight now and he can reach anything. He tries the handle – the door opens. The cupboard is full of exciting junk. He pokes around in it and finds a little green and red toy train, a spinning top, and a cloth book. Whose are these toys? Not his – they're baby toys. Carefully he puts them back as he found them and closes the door.

Taking care to avoid sanction he never spoke to Nain nor to anyone else about the toys. Over time the incident slipped into his subconscious – until now. Until one more piece of the jigsaw seemed to slip into place.

How was it, if Nain was so devout, Taid, Dad and the rest of the family had been so untouched by her religion? She must have lapsed when she married, or even before. But why had she returned to her faith? Could it be because of what happened to the little boy? Of course it could; this was what her affection for me was about. It always felt as if there was something in the way Dad and all his family related to me. Ah yes, but it was different with Mam. There was a coolness between her and them, a distance, despite living next door.

After all these years he saw his early life bathed in a different light. With a shock, he realised his growing up, the choices he'd taken, and the stories he'd told himself about why he did this or that, everything that led to the man he had become, was all happening, while in the eyes of the family he was supposed to be someone else. He felt he was changing, becoming his real self but, in so doing, the knowing was all. Who was his real self? He would have to face yet more questions before he could get an answer.

Chapter Nine

Llangollen, 1966

Gwyneth paused in the middle of getting ready to go off to work and watched Huw through the window of the front room. She smiled as he leapt the last two steps down to the pavement. Father and son are so alike; there was a prick of sadness, *were* so alike, she corrected. No scope for anxiety about the future nor for the conse-quences of their actions. *Huw seems quite happy going on his own without me each day, even though he's only seven.* It was not that far. From the front bedroom window, she could just make out the redbrick school among the blue slate roofs over the bridge. Herself next door said she would take him. Well, she would, wouldn't she, always pushing in and that. So she stood up to her and she wouldn't have her pick him up after school either. There was no need, she told her. She got home from the factory soon after him. But that didn't stop her wait-ing on the doorstep as she did.

Gwyneth stepped out and closed the front door. She had never been comfortable living next door to Emrys' parents. In fact, she hadn't wanted to come here. But it was only for the time being, he said. Just so they could keep an eye on things. It was simply to see if she was all right and to help out now and again until they could get a decent house over the river, not this poky hole with one tap and no bathroom. Well it hadn't worked out like that. It was nearly three years since Emrys' death. Three years making do by taking the job in the aircraft factory and of having to put up with Mary herself's meddling. And what gall! What treachery! Trying to impose her religion on Huw. How sly could you get? Showing him those pictures hanging on the wall and telling him all about their meaning. Leading him from one to the other like that. Each day waiting at her door for him coming from school. 'Just until you come home,' she'd said. But what else could be done? She couldn't get home until six. As for taking him to church – *that* church of all places. On a weekday after school, at that. Well, why hadn't she brought up her own children in her faith? Emrys had never been near a catholic church, neither had his brothers or sister. She should talk to her and put a stop to it. But what could she do? She lived next door to her and it had to be admitted she had no one else near at hand to turn to for help with Huw.

Gwyneth joined the queue pressing on behind when the bus turned in at the stop. As usual it was packed upstairs and down with people standing, so she stayed on the crowded rear platform. As it pulled away, she grasped the rail, hanging on with an ability born of practice. Well, she hoped Mary didn't give Huw biscuits again when he came home. The over-indulgence was irritating, and the cuddling and kissing. She forced herself to stop thinking about it.

Gwyneth stepped nimbly off the double-decker as it pulled into the long line of works buses. She allowed herself to be swept along in the torrent of people flowing through the gates and down the driveway. They were like ants, she thought, going into the immense nest that was the factory. On her first day, the scale of it had astonished her. Hordes of women in scarves and men in caps: an exodus making its way each day from the towns and villages of North Wales and the English border. Despite this, she was surprised at the comfort she derived from being one of the crowd, stepping out with a sense of common purpose. Immediately she entered the factory, she was enveloped by the rattle of the rivet guns, the screech of the air drills, and the cacophony of sound from the machinery. It reverberated within the cosmos of the vast enclosed space battering the core of her being. Something that would remain with her at home and in her sleep for many years to come. On her first day, as she passed through the enormous doors onto the main assembly floor, she had paused in shock. Met by her superintendent, she was taken to the training school where over the next few weeks she acquired the skills she needed. She also learned that the assembly line was a kilometre long. Given a time card, with her works number and name on it, she was told that it was an imprisoning offence to cheat the clock. The card was printed with time boxes and days and the machine punched neat holes exactly in the appropriate box. She took this card from the rack five times a week, punching in and out at the clocking station, marking her time at the factory.

Going to the workplace, she took her smock from her locker, put it on, and threw the switch on her machine. The work was repetitive. The capstan lathe was the master whose insatiable demands had to be met. Feed the steel bar into the machine. Shape the component. Part it from the bar. Repeat over and over throughout her shift in a steady unbroken rhythm of unconscious movement. The cutting fluid soaked her arms up to the elbows; wearing gloves and rolling up sleeves was forbidden because of the danger of moving parts. The vapour of the hot fluid burned her throat. Her back and legs ached from continually standing in one position on the unyielding concrete floor. But to Gwyneth it seemed there was a beauty in the work and in the exact detail required in operating the machine. It made a human action perfect to an accuracy of one tenth of a millimetre as she guided the capstan arm as fluently as if it was an extension of her own. Gradually she had found her body had been enveloped by a rhythm she would have found alien just three years before taking this job, in her previous life tied to the home.

However, while she was aware of her actions controlling the machine with surprising precision, closed within herself she allowed her thoughts to wander.

She hadn't wanted to call him Huw.

The idea arose as a mere jot in the continuum of the workplace routine. Emrys pressed her. She knew his mother was behind it. That woman ruled her family, sitting at the head of her kitchen table, determined to have her way in everything. What exactly *had* happened to

Mary's little boy? Scalded, she knew, but how? And what events led up to it? 'Scalded,' Emrys would say, little more than that.

There was a deep collective family grief that forbade the raising of any questions. So deep it spread its impenetrable mist over them all, imposing a conspiracy of silence that sought to exclude even herself. Perhaps to deny it had happened and thus to eliminate it. Perhaps also there was guilt. *Yes, that was it*, she thought. A desperate guilt that sought to turn back the events of that terrible day. To seek one more chance so the little boy might live. When Mary lost him, she was too old to have another. She can't let the dead child go. *She sees my Huw as the means of bringing him back to life*. The notion brought a shiver down her spine. Well, she would see that none of that reached him. They could have their silence but he must never know about the other Huw. The blast of the hooter signalled mealtime. She turned off her machine and pressed the red stop button with her knee. Two parts of the same action.

Chapter Ten

The clink of glasses jolted Cecil's attention. With a start he realised he'd finished most of the wine. *Oh dear. I seem to be inclined to drift into daydreaming lately. Maybe today's action has unsettled me. I must be getting too old for the job.* Perhaps Hackett's probing had been merited. Candles were flickering low at the tables as the gloom seeped in through the open street door. Darkness was closing in on the town. The idea of a stroll around before turning in seemed attractive. *Maybe it would help me to unwind. I could do with that. It should be safe enough though it might be chilly.* He reached for his coat.

Turning right at the front door he started up the street. The air felt fresh on his face and he breathed in its cool dampness. He decided to keep to that part of the town. It appealed to him, though it never used to, seeming so old-fashioned back then, with its narrow lanes and alleyways between the old houses and cottages. It was little changed, unlike the main street with its brash shop signs.

Another shower had made the cobbles shine in the harsh light of the street lamps. Slanting elongated shadows were thrown on the walls, creating a black-and-white world. This was his element, territory he knew well, he felt comfortable and relaxed.

Then, there was a footfall; he froze. It was light but enough for him to detect above the sound of traffic muted by distance and the gentle rushing of the river nearby. His surroundings changed as he slowly peered around. No longer familiar, they had become dystopian, threatening, out of joint. He'd become a stranger on a deserted Welsh street. In the blackness of an alcove there was the tip of a shoe caught in a faint patch of light. The headlights of a four-by-four crawling warily around a corner swept the alcove for a moment briefly, illuminating a face he recognised instantly. It was slacker, slightly jowled, but there was no doubt in his mind. It was Voronov.

In an instant they exchanged looks, both acknowledging each other across the distance of time. As he started towards him, the vehicle moved slowly between them drawing a long trailer and forcing him to step back. When it had passed, the alcove was empty. Voronov had gone, shielded by the vehicle and trailer, but where to?

He made off after the sound of retreating footsteps hastening on the cobbles, echoing and re-echoing in the narrow confines. Then he came upon a small square with four lanes leading from it. Impossible to tell in which direction the footsteps were going. He was left standing as they receded into silence. His mind was racing as he made his way slowly and cautiously in the direction of the hotel.

Was it Voronov or was it an illusion? If it was him, why had he made off like that? As he reached the hotel, he felt a sudden cold awareness of being followed. Slowly, he turned, squinting into the gloom. If there was someone, they seemed to merge into the shadowy darkness. It was just nerves, he told himself.

As he was preparing for bed by the light glowing weakly through a dusty shade he caught his face reflected in the dressing table mirror. Unsettled he leaned toward it examining his features. *Is this Huw,* he thought. *Did he look like this?*

He was a little boy falling through the mirror into a cemetery. There was Mrs Lottie Williams-Parry pointing into an open grave. In it was a tiny corpse its face covered by a white cloth. He leaned into the grave and drew it back. His own face looked up at him.

He awoke with a start soaked in sweat.

Chapter Eleven

Next morning as he stepped out into the keen air on his way to the newsagents he was still shaken by his dream and disturbed to realise how it revealed the extent to which he identified with his predecessor.

'Yes. Here it is, Mr Smith.' The man reached under the counter and handed the paper over.

'Thank you.'

'You're not the only one who likes to read that Russian paper this week. It's funny I go all year without any call for foreign papers, not even when the Eisteddfod's on, an' two of you come along at once, see.'

'What do you mean?' Cecil tried to appear as casual as possible, though his heart skipped a beat.

'Well I had it there an' this man came in this morning. I think he knows you.'

'Oh?'

'Yes. A foreign chap, he was. He looked foreign too, about your height, and getting on a bit. The paper was on the counter with the others and he asked me had it been specially ordered. Well, I told him "yes, as a matter of fact." He asked would it be a Mr Smith, by any chance? I thought, no 'arm in telling him, like, so I said "yes." Then he asked for a map from the rack there and when I went for it he started turning the pages of the paper as bold as brass. As if he could read it. I told him it was a special order, the only one I've got. He folded it up and put it back. I put it under the counter before the whole bloody town came in for a free read.'

'A local map?'

'What?'

'Was it a local map?'

'Yes. Ordnance Survey, the Explorer type.'

'Could you show me?'

The newsagent reached over to a display rack. 'One of these, it was.'

Cecil looked at the title, *Wrexham and Llangollen*. The frontispiece photograph showed a view of the Eglwyseg Escarpment. It was as familiar to him as his own face in the shaving mirror.

'Thank you.'

He tried to keep his hand steady as he paid and left. Back in his room he unfolded the *Izvestia* newspaper and turned the pages until, as he expected, he came to an envelope bearing his name in the Cyrillic alphabet.

Chapter Twelve

A peaty wind was coming from the south-west, aggravating the stiffness in Cecil's knee, so he eased it with a sip of the Whyte & McKay. He'd placed himself in the shadow of an overhang with the face of the scarp behind. This was the landmark Voronov had identified for the meeting. It was a natural passing place hewn out of the face of the great limestone escarpment by the quarrymen over a century ago with a hundred metre drop on one side. There was room for two cars to pull off the narrow track. To his left, a cleft in the face formed a crevasse with the muddy bed of a rust-brown stream containing barely a trickle of hard water. It led up to a plateau of sheep-cropped turf fifteen metres above. His own car was placed in a deep lane back beyond the escarpment. He'd come prepared after a good breakfast, with a packet of oat cakes and a small bottle of mineral water thrust in his coat pocket. He'd also made sure both his phones were charged before pocketing the charger to bring with him.

Casting his eyes up the uneven rocky wall towering to the clear blue sky, it was as he remembered it. *Why shouldn't it be*, he thought. Pitted and scored with ten thousand-year-old glacial patterns as it is. *I didn't know the cause of those brutal corrugations then.* He remembered the sense of insignificance the great face engendered in him over forty years earlier. As a boy he'd clambered on the rock shelves, spending nights alone in the open with the evening light forming sinister shapes in the pitted marks. Sometimes there was a visage with an awful expression. Sometimes a great head of some beast. Near the top was a huge lichen-encrusted fissure with foliage hanging from it.

He recalled that primordial anxiety long ago when, in the failing light of evening, going to the stream for water, it looked like a gigantic bear climbing the face.

Voronov doesn't know any of this, nor his seekers. Hopefully it should give me some advantage if it becomes necessary. Looking down the track from where he expected Voronov to come he strained to hear a motor, aware of the absolute stillness and solitude as he filtered out the sounds impinging on his sharpened senses. There was the plaintive call of a curlew, the bleat of a ewe, and the croaking of two ravens in the woods below Dinas Bran. It rose in the distance against the blue backdrop of the Berwyn hills. Sheep and cattle were like black and white jewels on the green pasture below and the plume of smoke from a steam train on the heritage railway drifted along the valley. Then his eye was caught by the skittering wings of a kestrel. He watched it rise high overhead. All of a sudden it screamed out an alarm call to its mate.

He saw the car before he heard it. There was the flash of the windscreen and a wisp of white dust. Voronov was coming. Was he alone? Was he being followed? Cecil clambered up the crevasse, ignoring the sharp pain in his knee. Slipping and cursing on the ochre-coloured clay, he scrabbled on the loose stones to the top of the cliff. Then he lay out on the turf overlooking the passing place and waited as the car approached.

It slowed then started to speed up, before slowing down again. *It's Voronov, sure enough*, he thought. *He's expecting to see my car pulled over, that's why he's hesitating.* The car rolled cautiously into the passing place and stopped with a creak of the handbrake. Shielding his eyes from the sun, Cecil looked down the track as it twisted its way around the scarp into the hazy distance some three kilometres away. There was nothing else in sight. The engine was turned off, drawing his attention back. After an expectant stillness, the door unlatched. It opened just a little as if the former KGB agent was sniffing the air for danger, then he got out, stretching himself to his full height. He wore only a light cotton jacket. Not heavy enough to keep out the keen mountain breeze nor to conceal a weapon. *It must be in his waistband, a belt holster.* Glancing towards the edge of the drop, Voronov walked around the car and spotted the crevasse. Guessing immediately where Cecil was, he leaned his back on the side of the car and looked up at the ridge calling out, 'Huw!' His voice echoed back to him off the rock face.

Cecil spoke softly in Russian, knowing what he said would be carried on the still air, 'Lev, go back around the car and put your hands on the roof – slowly.'

Voronov did as Cecil's disembodied voice told him, lifting his light-blue eyes up to the ridge and squinting at the sun falling on his face, enhancing his high cheek bones and his pock-marked skin.

Cecil stood up, revealing himself, Glock in hand. '*Zdravstvuyte*, Lev.'

Voronov paused for a moment and nodded as if appraising the situation before answering in English, 'It's been a long time, Huw.'

Voronov hasn't changed much. Not so lightly built now, a little stocky, hair still full but it's become snow-white. His eyes are still sharp as a viper's, though, and as shifty as ever. He carries something about him different from the old Voronov, the way his shoulders droop, the tension in his voice. I'm looking at a frightened man: frightened and dangerous.

'Why were you following me the other night, Lev?'

'Look, my friend, I'm going to get a stiff neck gazing up at you like this. Come on down. Yes?' He lifted his hands in a gesture to emphasise his words.

'Put your hands back.' *I'll get him up with me, separate him from his car while keeping close to mine and at the same time keep watch along the road.*

Voronov shrugged. 'OK. OK.'

Cecil lowered the pistol. 'For a man of your age, you ran well the other night, Lev,' he called. 'Why did you do it?'

'Why did you run out on me back in Berlin, Huw? You left me in a sticky situation with the material. I was lucky to hide it before my people caught up with me. As far as you were concerned I was finished, expendable.'

Cecil ignored Voronov's complaint. 'Where is it now, Lev?' He raised his pistol again.

47

Voronov smiled. 'You've come on your own, I see, otherwise you wouldn't keep pointing that gun at me.'

'Take out your weapon and hold it up above your head.'

Voronov shrugged again and reached for his waistband.

'Slow, Lev. Slow.'

He drew out the pistol holding it between fingers and thumb, his hand open.

'Place it on the ground.'

He did as he was told.

'Kick it under the car.'

Carefully pushing it out of sight with his foot, Voronov turned and called up to him, 'Satisfied?'

'Come up here.'

Panting somewhat and rubbing at some streaks of mud on his trousers, he reached the top of the crevasse and approached Cecil.

Swiftly, Cecil closed up to him, placing the muzzle of the Glock against Voronov's temple while he quickly made a contact search. Satisfied, he stepped back a few paces. 'Let's get from the edge, shall we?' He gestured with the pistol. 'Over there.' Then he slid his weapon into its holster.

They moved over to an outcrop capped by turf, forming a miniature lawn and low enough to provide seating overlooking the valley.

'Make yourself comfortable,' he invited, 'while I sit here.' He put some space between them. 'We might as well enjoy the view.'

Voronov took out a pack of cigarettes and, turning his back on the light breeze, conjured up a flame. Twisting round to him he blew out the smoke through the corner of his mouth and swept his cigarette hand to indicate the prospect. 'I could see this rock face from the town and I used one of those maps. What do you call them?'

'Ordnance Survey maps.' Cecil indulged him. 'You bought it at the newsagent's.'

'Yes. Very good. Well. I needed somewhere to meet you near the town but secure,' he pointed down the track, 'where I could see trouble coming.'

'You chose well.' Cecil watched him closely. There was a tense pause. 'What kind of trouble?'

With one hand, Voronov reached in his jacket pocket and took out small folding field glasses, training them on the track in the far distance. He drew on his cigarette and looked out at the expanse of scenery, as if pondering, before turning back to Cecil. 'I thought I could bury myself here where they couldn't find me – my people, you know? Your people shadowed me constantly. I didn't mind that. It suited me after I contacted them. I'd told them I'd hide up, waiting for you to make your move. But my people – I thought I'd shaken them off at Victoria. I jumped off a bus at some traffic signals and made it to the coach station. I'd already booked a seat on a coach for here, you see, having looked through the British guide books. Scotland too far, the north also, but going west . . .' he shrugged. 'This place, it's wild enough to shake them off, I thought, but not too far from London to get back without using the train. You know what railway stations are like: eyes everywhere. Now, where I have my room, people have called giving my description. You know how it goes – friends looking to meet up. So my people have followed me here.' He shrugged and smiled.

'They've followed me too, Lev.'

The smile on Voronov's face froze. 'So!'

'They tried to take me out in a village just north of here. They probably thought you were there too. They must have followed me over here to get to you.'

In an instant Voronov's mood changed. He stood up, turning to focus his field glasses on the track in the far distance as if he was expecting something. Intending to take another pull at his cigarette, he stopped. Instead, he tossed it away, turning to Cecil. 'You want to know what kind of trouble? I think you're going to find out.'

Chapter Thirteen

'How likely is it for a vehicle to come along here, do you think?' Voronov's voice was tense.

'Unlikely during the week.' Cecil moved toward him and looked over his shoulder following his line of vision and squinting into the sun. 'The car you came in,' his lips were almost touching Voronov's ear, 'yours?'

'Borrowed it unofficially,' he answered out of the side of his mouth, his glasses still trained on the vehicle now clearly visible, leaving a trail of white dust.

'You're going to have to leave it,' Cecil muttered. 'They'll have guessed you're up here to meet me. They're hoping to bag the two of us. My car is nearby. Come on.'

'Not before I get my pistol!' Voronov exclaimed, pocketing the glasses.

'There's no—' Before Cecil could complete his sentence, Voronov dashed for the crevasse with surprising agility and scuttled down. Cecil turned to look at the vehicle making its way along the track. It was a four-wheel drive with at least two people inside, maybe more. He heard Voronov scrabbling back up the crevasse before he reappeared. 'Come on. This way.' He made off for the lane across the plateau with Voronov following. Both of them breathing heavily. With Cecil hobbling, and ignoring the needling pains in his knee, they reached his car.

Chapter Fourteen

Voronov clutched the edge of his seat as Cecil pushed the screaming engine to the limit, with the old Honda snaking from side to side along the loose dirt of the twisting lane. The sessions at the police driving school came in handy after all.

Voronov shouted, 'Where are we going?' The rear of the car swung out on a precipitous bend scattering loose stones to fall a hundred metres to the valley below.

'I'm trying to shake them off,' Cecil shouted back at him, 'hoping they'll expect us to go for the A5 on the other side of the river and head east for London. That's why we're going west to a place I know on top of the moors. It'll give us time to work out what we're going to do.'

'So! You know this area. How?'

'Just trust me.'

'Ha!'

Twisting and turning over moorland, the lane came to a ford. Cecil swung the car off onto a rough quarrymen's trail along a stream and pulled up behind a hedge of furze screening it from the lane. 'Get out,' he ordered.

Voronov looked around and quickly sized up the situation. They were in a narrow gorge with a limestone rock face on either side rising up by a series of turf-carpeted terraces to high ridges lined with pines. The croaking of crows echoed from the rock faces as they circled against the narrow strip of blue sky above.

'Come on. Follow me.' Cecil limped ahead. They went on foot

up the steep trail to the head of the gorge and clambered up the chaos of loose scree shattered from the rock by millennia of frosts, until they reached a shelf blasted out of the face a century ago. He pointed to the track below. 'Nobody's going to come up here for a while. It looks as if your friends have headed off east. This gives us some time to work out what we're going to do, but not much.'

'What do you mean "what we're going to do"? You take me to your people now. It's what we're going to do. Yes?'

Cecil took his time selecting a place on a grassy bank free of rocky outcrops and sat down. He gestured encouragingly for Voronov to join him. Instead, the Russian remained standing, tense, alert. His eyes were darting restlessly from the cliff wall on one side of the gorge down to the track and up to the high ridge on the other side. Cecil moved his right hand close to his waistband holster. When Voronov turned back, he saw the Glock pointing at his chest. Cecil spoke in Russian. 'Sit down, Lev.'

Voronov lowered himself to the turf and took a sitting position, looking up warily.

'Keep your hands on the grass behind you.'

He complied.

Cecil moved his trigger finger outside the guard and returned to English. 'Now just relax, Lev, and listen to what I've got to say.' He took out his iPhone and held it up. 'Though your people don't know where you are right now, mine know where I am, even though this phone is switched off, and they're using me to get to you. They'll be asking why I've come up here and why my signal is static. I don't know where they are. They closed the shop after I met them the day before yesterday but they won't be far and if we just sit, they'll be here in less than an hour. All you have to do is say where the material is. When they pick it up that's it. Citizenship, money, and so on. Yes?'

Voronov cocked his head to one side, slightly querulous, almost insolent. 'So?'

'Do you know what's on that microfilm?'

Voronov's expression remained fixed. He gave a non-committal shrug.

'Of course you do and they know it. They can never be certain you haven't made copies, can they?'

'So?' he said it again but not so insolent that time.

'All transactions will have to take place in this country. Once they're done, you won't stay alive for long. They can't afford to have you free to enjoy your citizenship and money. If I hand you over, you go to your death – not immediately perhaps, but later for sure.' Cecil paused for effect. 'But I can't believe you haven't worked that out some time ago.'

'Sure I have.' Voronov's head twitched to one side, 'but I'll take my chances.'

He shifted nervously, moving his hand towards his waistband.

Cecil tensed and lifted the pistol with his finger curling round the trigger.

'Cigarette,' Voronov pointed to his pocket. 'Can I?'

Cecil took aim at his head. 'First take your gun out and put it down behind you – slowly.'

Voronov did as he was told. 'A cigarette now?'

Cecil nodded his permission, taking note of the way Voronov's hands trembled as he lit up. As he released smoke from his lungs, Cecil compared his features with those of the man he had known. *His past is written on his face and neck*, he thought. The skin is slacker now, more drawn around his mouth and, by the way his Adam's apple moves up and down, he's anxious too. He took out the Whyte & Mackay bottle. 'We're not so different are we, Lev, you and I?'

Voronov took another deep pull on his cigarette and released the smoke upwards before looking at him from the corner of his eyes.

Cecil poured a measure into the cap and took a sip. 'Both lone wolves, both recruited at university, your wife gone, like mine, no children.' He took another sip. 'When was it we came up against each other? Berlin ninety-five? Two young lads, green as grass, so naïve. Those were the days.' He drained the cap. 'What happened to you to bring you back in the game? Don't tell me. Let me think. The authorities shuffled through the old KGB files and the material was rediscovered. They worked out you had it and had kept it to yourself. After that, they must have set the SVR on to you. They would've called you in for a chat. You couldn't have been arrested or you wouldn't be here now. Oh, I know what it must have felt like, to be yanked back. So they let you go for the time being but you knew that was only the opening bout. They would come for you when it suited them. They'd drag you in and force it all out of you before the bullet in the back of the neck.' He sighed. 'Now, after all these years, we're both back.' He offered the bottle to Voronov.

Voronov leaned forward and accepted it. He drew on his cigarette again, slowly releasing the smoke. Taking a mouthful, he rolled it around his tongue. 'After I was called in for a chat, as you say, I suppose I could see no further than getting out.' He drew on the cigarette again. 'Have you ever spent time in the Yasenevo headquarters?'

Cecil acknowledged the question with a sympathetic roll of his eyes.

Voronov took another mouthful before handing the bottle back. 'I could see no further than getting to the UK and making some sort of a deal. Oh, I knew it was dangerous but I was just buying time.'

Cecil put the bottle away. 'So why were you *really* coming to meet me today, Lev?'

As if to gain time to rehearse his answer, Voronov moved his position on the turf and stubbed the cigarette out on a rock. 'I wanted to see what would happen when my . . .' he struggled for the English word, 'seekers came along.'

'You mean you knew they would follow you? That was a bold, or should I say, a desperate move.' Cecil looked at him for some moments. 'And pretty treacherous too. You led them to me.'

'That's it, Huw, my friend. I had to find out if you were in this town to do a deal with them or with me.'

'And that's really why you dived down to retrieve your gun.'

Voronov shrugged. 'I wasn't sure you would go for your car or just hand me over so I had to be ready. When I came back up I was in a position to deal with you and, of course, them. But as it worked out, you ran for it, so I decided to stick with you as you're my best card. You were a lucky man today. One false move and—'

'And the other night in the town, why were you following me?'

'I needed to find out if you were setting out to meet them. For all I knew a trade-off had been struck between both sides. It wouldn't be the first time, you know that.'

Cecil nodded in acknowledgement. 'You ran away because I'd seen you?'

'Yes. The whole thing was a failure. It proved nothing. After some thought, I decided on the meeting today to, how would you say, bring us all together?'

'It was a hell of a risk. If the SVR had got you today they'd have taken you back to their laboratory in the Russian embassy and squeezed you dry before the bullet in the back of the neck.'

'So! You think I don't know? You would have had a bullet too, my friend, and while we're talking about it, how do you know your people won't do the same to you once they have what they want?'

Cecil changed his position on the grass. 'That's a good question.' He indicated to Voronov he could retrieve his pistol and returned the Glock to its holster. 'You're right. I don't know. My feeling is it's likely they will do the same to me, as you suggest.'

Voronov slipped the weapon into its waistband holster. Clasping his hands around his knees he leaned back, his head on one side, saying archly, 'You know you can always go to the police if you think you're in danger.'

Cecil returned his remark with a mock disdainful glare. 'Thanks for the advice, Lev. Perhaps *you'd* like to call them.'

Voronov remained looking at him, still holding his arch smile.

'When you contacted my people in London, you said you had the microfilm with you. Where is it now, Lev? I can't believe you've left it behind back there?'

The smile left his face. There was no answer.

'You've brought it with you, haven't you?'

'I haven't got it with me, but,' he shrugged, 'I have information about it not far from here.'

55

'In the town?'

'*Da*. In the town.' Looking back at Cecil, Voronov shrugged again. 'I've deposited it as insurance.' Abruptly he changed tack. 'So! According to you, I don't sell it to your people, I give it to you for yourself. Why?'

'The information on that microfilm should be out in the public domain, on the internet, social media and so on.'

'Hah!' Voronov stood up. He was shivering. The sun was now failing to find its way into the gorge and there was a cooling chill in the air. He turned away from Cecil, his eyes taken by a hen harrier flashing its way across the rock face. Still with his back to him, Voronov addressed his words to the escarpment across the gorge.

'Let me get this straight: you want me to take you to the microfilm so that we can go public with it instead of doing a deal with your people.' Voronov turned back to him. 'Is that so?'

Cecil offered no response.

'And how would we do it? If we went to the newspapers, they'd go straight to the authorities. We can't put it on disk, we haven't got the equipment to digitise it to the appropriate format, unless you know someone. Do you?'

Still Cecil was silent, remaining seated and looking up at him.

'No, you don't. And anyway if we went to a specialist company with that stuff on it – no.' He took a step towards Cecil. 'And another thing: how do I know this isn't your way of getting hold of it and handing it over, me as well? After all, that's what your orders are.'

Cecil ignored Voronov's question and spoke quietly, 'It was never just about citizenship, money and so on, was it, Lev?'

Voronov was clearly taken aback. 'What do you mean?'

'We both know what happened to those children at the Berlin Friendship House, their lives shattered – you especially – you know.'

Voronov tensed. 'Go on.'

'The Suvorov Military School in St. Petersburg, nineteen-seventy. How old were you, thirteen? Need I say more?'

Voronov seemed to shake himself momentarily. 'How do you know this, from my KGB file, an informer?'

Cecil still sitting on the turf leaned back on his elbows and looked up at Voronov, eyeing him intensely. 'Something like that.'

'And you knew this all along when we were negotiating back then?'

Cecil nodded once just slightly. He went on. 'That lecturer, what was his name? KGB Major Alexander Stasov. He was eventually found out, but not before he'd done incalculable damage to many young boys, including you. The scandal was suppressed, of course. He was posted to the command of the Berlin Friendship House, presumably where his talents could be more profitably employed by the KGB. But you already know that, don't you? You've always known it. As you rose up in the organisation you followed his career, shadowing him, waiting for a chance to – to what, Lev? Were you ever clear what you were going to do?'

Voronov remained silent, unmoving. A stillness had descended on him.

'Prosecutor Stepankov never got his hands on that film when Poltoranin's office was raided, did he? You'd already acquired it in the chaos that reigned in the Lubyanka under Yeltsin. You would use that film to destroy Stasov. But he died, cirrhosis of the liver, it was said, and you were left with dynamite ready to blow up in your face because they were still after it. Oh, they had a new name but they were still the old KGB boys and they would be asking some awkward questions if they traced it to you. Then things quietened down, the heat was off, until recently.'

Cecil got to his feet and took some steps to look over the gorge. He turned back to Voronov. 'So, after Stasov died, why didn't you just dispose of the film, dump it, burn it? You couldn't bring yourself to do it, could you? Somehow, it wasn't enough that Stasov was dead. You wanted justice for the evil he'd done – what he'd been responsible for. The game was on again. That's what brought us together in ninety-nine. You thought you were going to get a new life in the West and bring Stasov, and the evil of the Berlin Friendship House, out into the open.'

'You were good at persuading me to come over.'

'That's because I felt the same about the Berlin Friendship House, Lev.'

'It wasn't because of me that it fell through.'

'It fell through because I wanted it to, when I found out what was intended for the film. It was never going to see the light of day. But you still held on to it despite the danger – hoping, I suppose, for another chance; a rerun perhaps. Well this is it, Lev, a second chance. What do you say?'

Voronov spoke softly, 'I think what you say about your people and mine is possibly true but if, and it's a big if, we *were* able to get the information out on the internet, it would be the end of me and of you, for certain. I don't like to say this but for you it's best to hand me in to your people. I take my chances.'

'Once it was out in the public domain, no longer secret, those who were exposed would immediately become helpless. Their power would melt away and no one would want to be associated with them or dare to touch us in their name. The evidence is too graphic to be denied. These things are on people's minds now. There's more aware-ness of the evil of it. Look, it's our only chance of surviving this. We've got to make a move. Time is running out.' He gave an urgent edge to his voice. 'My people are probably on their way even now, so if we stay here you'll be meeting them shortly, whether you want to or not.' He looked up at Voronov, deliberately allowing the tension to build before he spoke again. 'Now this is how it is: I'm prepared to go on the run, the two of us, and we get that stuff from wherever you've stashed it.'

'Then what? We'll have my people and yours after us, so what good will that do?'

'If *we* have it, we have some control over our future. Don't you see that, Lev? Once they have it, we're both finished. Make up your mind.' Cecil got to his feet and pointed down the track. 'They'll be coming up that lane in minutes. When they get to the ford we're blocked in, with no way out.'

Voronov stood up clasping his hands around his arms attempting to rub the chill from them. 'Cecil, you bastard! So you may be right. What can we do?' He was shivering now. His thin cotton jacket was clearly inadequate.

Now is the time to soften Voronov up. To use those skills I'm supposed to be good at, Cecil thought. He shrugged off his coat and, after transferring the contents of the pockets to his jacket, he tossed it to Voronov. 'Here, before you freeze to death.'

Gratefully, Voronov put it on as Cecil said, 'Look, I'm going down to the car with or without you. If you're with me, we'll go north up this track and over the hills, keeping my people behind us. As I said before, I know these moors like the back my hand. We can lose them and circle round back to Llangollen. I'll plant this phone on a truck going south and with luck that should put them off the scent for a short while. It won't fool them for long but it'll give us time to get the microfilm. We can hide up out of town while we figure out what to do next.'

Voronov stood with his head to one side. He was hesitating.

'If you're not with me by the time I get to the car, I'll report in and say you broke and ran for it. You'll be singing your heart out to them within twenty-four hours and on a slab in forty-eight. As for me, well, I'll have to accept that they get the microfilm to do with as they will and hope my chances of staying alive are more than fifty-fifty. If you stay with me, they'll know I'm not bringing you in. They've probably worked it out by now anyway. We'll both be on the run together.' He turned his back on Voronov and set off down the track.

When Cecil reached the car, Voronov shouted, 'Hey, Huw, you crazy bastard! Wait for me.' But not before Cecil froze. He caught the sound of a powerful engine at full revs. A four by four coming from the direction of Llangollen: Hackett. Signalling for Voronov to get down he plunged into the cover of the furze bushes screening the Honda. There was a slim chance they would speed past before their locator registered him. He could get Voronov to him and take off in the opposite direction down to the town before Hackett's men could turn round and come back. The vehicle swerved as it took the bend. Forced to slow down, it splashed through the ford swinging toward the furze bushes. Then, veering around and up the lane, it followed it over the moors giving Cecil a fleeting glimpse of the vehicle he'd seen before at the Eglwyseg Escarpment. 'Voronov's friends,' he muttered. 'So I haven't shaken them off.'

Chapter Fifteen

The temporary operations room in a disused police station somewhere in Oswestry, twelve miles from Llangollen in the North Wales borderlands

Arriving back from Birmingham, Hackett entered. There was a brief look of distaste as he took in the musty air of the room. It was his first time in the mildewed building. He hoped it would be his last. After glancing around, he moved over to the equipment and, leaning over Kerr sitting at it, he looked at the plot on the screen. Shouldering Kerr aside, he brought up the Ordnance Survey map overlay. 'If your plot's correct, he's been stopped for three hours here,' he pointed. 'Somewhere below that escarpment, about four miles north of the town. Does his car trace agree with this?'

Kerr nodded. 'After leaving the town going north-west, he went on what must be a lane on the other side of the castle mound. Then he stopped for a while before he moved off to where he is now.'

'He's made a contact, that's what he's done – but why has he not called us in and why has he moved on to this place? We've no one on the ground in the town itself. The Russians will have arrived there by now and possibly had him under observation. We need to bottle him up.' Turning to Kerr, he demanded, 'You've acted on this?'

'Yes. Lessing has two of our people ready to go up the track from the Llangollen side and two approaching down the track from over the moors to the north-west here,' he indicated on the map, 'ready to close in.'

'And they've got the appropriate weapons for open moorland?'

Kerr hesitated. 'Sir?'

'Just in case. You know what I mean,' Hackett was impatient, 'rifles, a marksman.'

'Yes. They're equipped.'

'Do it now. Find out what's going on. Approach with caution. He may be acting off the books. Have they all got a full description of Cecil, what he's wearing, so that he can be identified from a distance?'

'Yes but we don't know what Voronov's wearing.'

'Never mind Voronov. It's Cecil we may have to take out if he makes a run for it. Tell your men not to hesitate to do that but remember Voronov's no good to us dead. With luck we can hook him in.'

Chapter Sixteen

Throwing his phone through the open window, Cecil eased the car down the rocky trail. The suspension groaned and protested as he swung the car north onto the lane opposite to the way they had come. Putting his foot to the floor, he set the Honda's engine screaming at the steep climb out of the gorge. The way before them twisted and undulated over the moorland. The elderly Civic's rear veered from side to side with the tyres scrabbling for a hold on the loose uneven surface, shovelling clouds of limestone grit behind it.

He could hear Voronov cursing in Russian. 'Why are we going after them?'

'We have no choice. My people will be here at any moment,' Cecil shouted. 'We'll keep well back out of mirror sight. Your friends will probably get to the village before they realise they've lost us and come back. There's a track ahead that will get us off their tail. It crosses this lane and circles round; we'll take that. Once your friends realise they've missed us and come haring back, hopefully they'll run straight into Hackett's men.'

They never saw the four by four coming towards them until they breasted a rise coming out of a dip. The vehicles, with wheels locked, tobogganed toward each other, reducing speed in two banks of dust. Then they merged with enough impact to burst both radiators and send the poor Honda into a ditch.

Apart from a bruised feeling on his chest from the seatbelt, and confusion as to how the Russians' vehicle could have come back so quickly, Cecil didn't think he'd suffered anything of concern. The steam made it almost impossible to make out the occupants in the other vehicle but he could see a rifle between them. It must have been thrown forward with the impact. 'Out!' he shouted, flinging open the door and dragging a shocked Voronov through it. 'Follow me.' Voronov caught the urgency in his voice and, despite the whiplash pain in his neck, ran without question. They made for it up the rising ground to the east, stumbling awkwardly through the heather. As they reached the top with lungs bursting, a sharp crack seemed to rip the air sending a pair of red grouse rising from gorse bushes, wings furiously thrumming.

'Rifle! Get down!' Cecil shouted. But Voronov was already sprawled on his face.

Chapter Seventeen

Instinctively, Cecil flattened himself on the ground, facing the way they had come. He pressed his body into the loose grey soil. Drawing his pistol, he parted the sprigs of heather with the muzzle and peered through them, taking stock. With his other hand he eased his knee. Through the clouds of steam from both radiators, he could see the man with the rifle was helping his companion out of the vehicle. It appeared he had been stunned in the crash. The sun caught the weapon. It was a Heckler and Koch G36, standard issue to the Security Services. So, it was Hackett's men and not the Russians, Cecil realised. *They must have got onto the lane from the track ahead and missed each other. With the illuminated telescopic sight, the shot was a snip at the two hundred metres we'd put between them and us. It wasn't a wild shot. Oh no. It was the coat, my coat, giving priority to the target. A dead Voronov was no good to them. The shooter believed he was taking me out.*

The thought turned Cecil's blood cold.

Taking aim at the vehicle he squeezed off one round as a suppressing shot. At that range he knew he had little chance of hitting any of them but it would keep their heads down for a brief while. With the pistol pointing down to the track, he rolled lengthwise over and over to Voronov. He could see the shot had taken him in the lower back to the side. It was not good. Gently he eased him over. The coat was open, revealing a widening mass of gore on his chest. Cecil ripped his shirt open and saw the ugly exit wound gaping purple and black with blood pumping out. He put his gun down and pressed his hands on it but he knew nothing could be done as the blood spread around and through his fingers, warm and viscous. Voronov's eyes were open the lids fluttering. Cecil put his mouth close to his ear. 'Can I do something for you, Lev?'

His lips moved. He was speaking Russian. 'It's burning. God, it's burning.'

Wiping his crimson hands on Voronov's shirt, Cecil pulled the field pack from inside his jacket. Breaking it open he took out the fentanyl lozenge on its stick and eased it between Voronov's lips gently pushing it up inside his cheek, saying in Russian, 'This will help, Lev. Just give it a few minutes.' He turned back to look down the slope through the bracken. They'd taken cover behind the cars.

Turning back to Voronov Cecil could see the fentanyl was doing its work, though his fingers were fluttering over his chest. Checking his breathing, Cecil spoke closely in his ear, 'Can you hear me, Lev?'

Voronov nodded, his face turned up to the sky.

Cecil drew the stick from his mouth. Still speaking in Russian, he said, 'In case you don't make it, Lev, tell me where the microfilm is.'

Voronov's lips moved, soundlessly at first, then a weak but clear voice pleaded, 'Get me some help, Huw.'

'Tell me, Lev, then help will be on the way.'

Voronov's breathing slowed. Cecil replaced the stick and turned to the track. The man with the rifle had taken a position in the ditch, the other was probably behind the cars. *They're waiting for more help before they make their move.*

Cecil murmured in his ear, 'Lev.'

Voronov turned his face to him.

'Can you hear me, Lev?' Cecil took the lozenge from his mouth.

Voronov's hand seized his jacket collar in a desperate grip. 'Help me, Huw.'

'The microfilm, Lev,' Cecil was becoming frantic, 'tell me, then I'll get help.'

Voronov's hand slipped from his collar.

Cecil cursed under his breath. *He mustn't leave me now, not before he tells me.* 'It's in that room of yours, isn't it?'

Voronov shook his head weakly.

'Where then?'

His eyes were filming.

Trying to restrain his mounting frustration, Cecil shook him gently. 'Where, Lev, where?'

Voronov was going. Cecil felt the anger rising from deep inside him. *He can't leave me now, the treacherous swine.*

His eyes half closed, his head lolling to one side, with rattling breath, Voronov rasped in English, 'The shop.' Then he was gone.

Cecil heard a car coming at speed from the direction of Llangollen. There was a screech of brakes. Peering through the heather, he saw two men leap from the vehicle and make for the ditch to join their comrades. *They'll soon form a crescent and move toward me to flush me out,* he thought. *I need to be off. Should I take my coat back . . . it's going to be a cold night? No. With luck they'll pass Voronov's body in pursuit with no immediate reason to check it. They'll keep thinking I'm Voronov and hold their fire.*

Using the front of the coat still wrapped around Voronov, Cecil cleaned the rest of the blood off his hands and wrists. He unclipped Voronov's waistband holster with its pistol, a Makarov nine millimetre Russian security services standard issue. Then he checked the magazine and thrust it in his jacket pocket. A search of Voronov's pockets brought forth a card for a walkers' hostel in the town and the folding field glasses which he thrust in his jacket but nothing else. A further search of Voronov's jacket lining brought no result. Cecil turned the body over on its face so they would still think it was he. A look at his watch gave him an hour of midsummer light before it started to fail. He needed to be away over the ridge and across the moor to the east to shake off any pursuit before he decided what to do next.

Making for the ridge, he rolled over the top so as not to present a silhouette. As he descended onto the flat moorland a scene familiar from his boyhood unrolled before him. It was the emerald-green stretch of the great moss. It always looked so innocent, so flat and inviting. But it was the graveyard of sheep and wild ponies. An idea flashed into his mind. It was desperate but there was just a chance. The *only* chance, as his knee would soon be slowing him down with the pain becoming persistent. He knew what he must do. Moving to the treacherous quaking sphagnum before they topped the ridge, instead of going straight on and into the bog, he turned to his side, changing direction. Stumbling on the dried heather stalks, he circled round putting the bog between himself and his pursuers.

Cecil stood on the higher ground where they could see him clearly and pulled his collar up so they wouldn't realise he wasn't Voronov. He could hear their calls as they topped the ridge in a ragged line and spotted him. He knelt down as if exhausted and spent. *Will it work?* It was more than he dared hope. Unsuspecting and thinking he'd just run across the open ground before faltering, three of them moved forward to close in on their prey. A fourth held back, speaking into his radio. At a signal the three broke into a run intending to rush him.

At first, they splashed through the margins of the moss, causing a flight of golden plover to rise up from feeding. Their beating wings scattered jewel-like drops of water. As the men reached the peaty surface, quaking and undulating with their footsteps, they broke through the sphagnum top, plunging in up to their knees. With arms flailing, they tried to keep their balance. Cecil stood up. He had no feelings for them though he knew there could only be one outcome. Unable to feel firm ground under his feet the man with the rifle dropped it and attempted to get back to the edge of the bog. He threw himself toward it, his arms thrashing as if he was attempting to swim. The fourth man dropped his radio and ran forward, sinking to his knees as he grasped a scrabbling outstretched hand. But his attempt was futile as the black morass enveloped the body of his comrade, snatching his hand away as he sank out of sight with a terrible obscene gurgling.

The others made no attempt to call or cry out as they desperately struggled to free themselves, sinking deeper and deeper into the squelching sucking mire. The bog closed over them one by one,

68

leaving only bubbling and popping in the mud-pools of the moss. As the fourth man scrambled clear of the bog and collapsed face down on the firm ground, the plover settled back to their feeding.

Now is not the time to deal with the survivor, Cecil thought. Others would be on their way and shots would attract them. He had to be off across the moor and onto higher ground. He turned his back on the bog to get his bearings from the distant lead mine workings. They were barely visible in the gathering dusk. That was why he failed to see the sinister forms of two men on the ridge silhouetted against the darkening sky. They were about to close in on him.

Chapter Eighteen

He was plodding, his legs feeling heavy, as the tufts of tough mountain grass pulled at his feet triggering flashes of pain in his knee. Then he heard it: a faint buzzing. *They've got a drone up. The drone would be sweeping the darkling moor with a thermal imaging camera,* he thought. *The mine workings, that's it! I must get to them before it comes my way.* The drone also sent the watchers scuttling across the moorland in the opposite direction seeking shelter back towards the lane. Cecil gathered new energy into his legs, staggering, half running, half stumbling, until he reached the derelict engine house with his heart thumping in his chest.

There it was. Still there after all those years. The collapsed arch in the massive structure, surrounded by fallen masonry, forming a man-made cave. He scrabbled his way through the gap between the top of the arch and the tumbled stones just as he'd done many times over forty years ago. This time his scrambling had a deadly purpose. The thermal imaging camera would never penetrate through the mass of stonework above him. He was safe for the time being.

Huddled among the collapsed masonry, he pulled his jacket around himself against the chill of the night air and tried to ignore the smell of sheep dung. Using the torch, he made a supper of oat cakes and water before bedding down for the night with his chin on his chest and dozed. Once or twice he thought he heard the drone sweeping and hunting across the night-shrouded moor. He strained his senses to listen but there was only the scream of a creature in its death throes and the sharp persistent cry of a fox. It was eerie and unsettling. As he was nodding off the screech of a short-eared owl woke him with a start and set his thoughts roaming around in his head. This was the first opportunity since Voronov's death that he'd had time to think.

By now Hackett will know they've killed Voronov instead of me so he'll continue to hunt me down. It's obvious he's bent on his assignment and prepared to go ahead under his own steam. Whether the Service are aware of this I'm not sure but, for now at least, I'm on my own. No technical support – or support of any kind. What to do next when I'm rested?

'The shop.' He recalled Voronov's final words. *It must be the newspaper shop. Where else? Has Voronov left something there? Hackett will expect me to attempt to return to Llangollen and search for the microfilm. It's a small town, so he should have no difficulty in having it covered and he'll have the hotel report my presence the instant I return. They'll be wondering where I am anyway.* Cecil knew that to the east, below the spur of moorland, lay a steep valley cut by the River Dee. Across it, on its hill, was the village. *That'll be the last place Hackett will expect me to go and it probably has an early opening convenience store where I can get food. Must take care to avoid the wrecked coffee bar, though. The drone has limited flying time in an operation, an hour maybe more depending on the type, and it will be seeking over the moor towards Llangollen. I just have to take a chance, cross the moor, and move down to the village. Then I can decide how and when to get to the town.*

Just before sleep crept up on him, he decided he would move off under the cover of darkness so that he would reach the river before first light.

After some hours, his watch told him it was time to scramble out and take a look at the sky in the east. It was still dark and getting to the river by first light was too dangerous. Instead, he held his position, keeping still and listening for the drone. Soon the first glimmer of dawn light appeared low on the eastern horizon, prompting the calls of curlews. Finishing the water in the bottle, he moved off down the spur walking into a light wind that wreathed him with damp chilly tendrils of mist. He knew that somewhere at the foot of the spur, if he could find it, was the old quarry that would help him get his bearings.

71

Suddenly a ghostly white form appeared before him in the dank early gloom. He froze, with his heartbeat held in suspension. A ewe sprang up with a startled mutter and trotted away. He realised he was on one of the many sheep tracks and if he followed it he would be led to the quarry and a pool used by the sheep as a source of water.

He almost tumbled over the edge of the diggings as a wisp of dank vapour cleared just in time. In the early light he went down into the great bowl gouged out of the moor by the steam digging machines decades ago. He recognised the pathways among the immense fossil encrusted blocks of stone left behind when the workings ceased. That was when he heard the drone.

Cecil knew there was a dynamite store somewhere among the chaos of the abandoned workings across the floor of the quarry. It was a small square column of thick concrete blocks forming a room, once panelled in wood, with a stout metal door, long since crumbled away. Roofed with thick dense concrete, it would be proof enough against the thermal imaging camera of the drone. Seeking cover among rusting machines and tumbled blocks of stone he made his way toward the store until, stiff with the chill gripping his body, he was able to hobble toward it across open ground as fast as he could.

Standing inside up to his ankles in sheep dung he heard his seeker gliding around the quarry. With a sibilant beat of its fan blades, it came nearer. Shrinking back against the wall in the darkness away from the doorway, he sensed it peering around corners and into apertures. Then it paused briefly before gliding off.

Moving to the doorway in the strengthening dawn light, he heard it lifting out of the quarry and on to the moor, still seeking. *It hasn't found me or it would be hurrying back to its masters*. It was safe to carry on for a short while at least but before that he would warm up in the first beams of the sun breaking over the quarry ridge.

Stumbling down the wooded slopes into the valley he could hear the river but first, he remembered, he would have to cross a narrow road. On the other side of it there used to be a car-breaker's yard. If it was still there, it would offer good cover down to the riverbank.

As he came through the trees he could just make out a shack nestled among the hulks of old cars rusting away in the coarse mountain grass. *So*, he thought, *the breaker's yard is still there.*

Crossing over the road, he stepped through the broken fencing without any trouble. The shack seemed empty and locked. There was no smoke from its stovepipe chimney. It was too early for any sign of life anyway. A narrow lane ran between crushed cars stacked high on either side, leading him down to a ford where the river was shallow at that time of year. He crossed without much difficulty, except for wet feet.

Moving along the river bank, he came to a familiar path he knew would lead up to a lane at the top of the village. Cecil paused in the cover of wild rhododendrons and looked back over the river from where he'd come, just to ensure there were no followers. But he failed to see the two leaf-dappled figures standing motionless in the shade of the wood. A glance at his watch showed just seven o'clock. A convenience store would be open. The lane joined the main street. It was almost deserted.

It was no trouble finding a store, where he bought a razor and shaving cream. He chose liquid gel soap for washing – he thought it would be easier to use in cold water – and he picked up a hand towel, sandwiches, and mineral water. Then he took them in a carrier bag back down to the river. Moving to a secluded spot, he stripped off completely and washed. Shivering, he dried himself in the keen air before shaving. After dressing, he breakfasted on the sandwiches, wolfing them down and surprising himself at his sudden hunger. He found a suitable boulder at the riverside and sat resting for an hour or so, until more people would be about.

Chapter Nineteen

He walked apprehensively along the main street thinking, *it's just as I always remembered it: lined with sooty red brick buildings.* It's coming to life now with people about, stepping out on their way to work. They're picking up their newspapers and buying their cigarettes. There's a woman pushing a buggy with one hand and holding a little fair-haired girl in the other. An elderly man is carrying a bottle of milk. Now he's paused to call to someone. People at a bus stop are looking on while a man is putting up a ladder. He looks like a painter. Or *is* he a painter?

A woman was sweeping her doorstep. As he passed she took up the doormat, shaking it vigorously. He sensed her pausing to stare ominously at his back for a moment before going on with her work. When he turned, she'd gone indoors.

Cecil had a feeling all was not as it seemed. *It's absurd, just nerves*, he thought, *understandable under the circumstances. I'm on-edge and need somewhere to stay, for one night at least. Just until my nerves have settled down while I work out how best to get into Llangollen. But first, I'll get out of this formal suit. It's obviously attracting attention.*

From a charity shop he bought a cheap-looking jacket to hide his shoulder holster, jeans, a couple of shirts, some underwear, trainers, and a holdall bag to carry his discarded clothes and newly bought toiletries.

By the beginning of the afternoon he was satisfied his appearance wouldn't invite any more stares. After getting some lunch in a squalid café in the upper part of the village he found a newsagent's window where, among the cards offering bikes for sale, handymen for hire, and home massage, he thought perhaps there would be a room advertised.

Then he sensed someone coming to stand beside him. It was a man also looking in the window, or so he thought until he realised his mistake. His heart dropped. He moved to escape but too late – the unmistakable muzzle of a pistol jabbed him in the ribs while a voice from behind whispered in Russian, 'Put hands in pockets. Keep them there and come with us.'

Chapter Twenty

His bag was taken by another man while an arm around his shoulder propelled him along the village street. They arrived at a corner and turned into an alley. He knew it well from the past. It joined a lane, sunken and secluded, leading past the cemetery and crossing the river to the old lead mine by an ancient stone bridge. *They must have shadowed me over the moors, somehow tracking me to the village. They've made the snatch in typical Russian style, either to complete the execution job that was intended before or to take me to a place of interrogation. This man at the side of me is young and half a head taller.* He couldn't see the owner of the hand holding his shoulder in a powerful grip. It was not looking good.

They turned off the alley into the sunken lane, with high banks and hedges, continuing along the length of the cemetery. *Oh Christ, this is an ideal spot for an execution.* But instead they stopped at the only car in the lane. *So, it seems I'm going for a ride.* The owner of the arm around his shoulder, still speaking Russian, told him to spread his feet and put his hands on the top of the vehicle. A large brutal palm cupped the back of his head and pressed his mouth to the side of the car. He could feel his teeth grating against the metal as his lips split and he felt the warm salt taste of blood. An efficient hand swept him, emptying the holster under his arm and placing the Glock on the car roof. Fishing out the Makarov in his waistband, he held it up for his companion to see and tossed it over to him.

Cecil's muzzle-jabbing companion went around to the driver's side and got in behind the wheel while his strong-armed captor thrust a pistol in his ribs. Cecil grunted with the pain. Then he heard a familiar voice.

'Hello. What's going on here then?'

He recognised it immediately. Many things seemed to happen at once. The Russian, distracted, relaxed the pressure on his head. At the same moment they both turned round. Miss Lottie Williams-Parry was standing at a small gate almost hidden by wild hawthorn bushes on the top of the bank on the cemetery side. Seizing his chance, Cecil spun around at the same time bringing the side of his clenched fist hard against the man's temple with all his might, slamming his head into the car roof. He showered blows on it in a terrible explosive frenzy before freeing himself from his captor's slackening arms, leaving him to slide to the ground. The realisation there was no way back now brought a dreadful resolve. He staggered around the front of the vehicle. The other Russian had his hand around the door opening it to spring out and deal with him. Cecil launched himself at the door panel, slamming into it with his shoulder driven by the full weight of his body. There was a scream as the Russian's hand was destroyed. Wrenching the door open again, Cecil grabbed the man's collar, pulling him so that his head was against the post and once again he hurled himself at the door. The skull made a sickening crunch as it burst. He went back to the other man. He was slumped forward on his knees against the car. Cecil kicked him in the side of his chest so he rolled on his back. He seemed to still be alive, though his face was covered in blood from a terrible wound on his forehead. Cecil retrieved his pistol but he couldn't take the chance of finishing him off with a shot. The last thing he wanted was for someone to hear it and call the police, so he placed his foot on the exposed throat and brought his full weight to bear on it. For some seconds there was a terrible rattling noise with hands grasping at Cecil's ankles as the Russian's voice box collapsed. Gradually all movement ceased, his hands fell away, and he was still, his bulging eyes staring at the sky.

Chapter Twenty-One

As Cecil holstered the Glock, a shadow fell on the road surface. He looked up with a start. Miss Lottie Williams-Parry was standing over him, holding her wallet open for him to see her warrant badge. Somehow she seemed different from before at the grave. The trousers and short coat she was wearing gave her a more severe look. She regarded the Russian lying in a pool of blood without flinching. 'You've made a bit of a mess here, haven't you? It's lucky I was in the cemetery. I've got a grave to check on, see.'

He stood up and, giving a cursory glance over her wallet, he nodded. 'I know about this.' His hand went back to the holster. *I wonder what she knows and what she's going to do next.* 'Have you been contacted since we last met?'

She shook her head.

He was surprised at how calm she was. He would play for time until he could make her out then he would have to deal with her one way or another.

'Your mouth's bleeding.'

He ignored the remark. 'I need to get rid of these without the emergency services.' He swept his hand loosely over the scene. 'Hide them or something.'

'Why? Aren't you going to get help?'

'It's important this is kept within the Service. So everything's left to me until I contact them later.' He watched her closely. *Is she accepting this story? If so, I can make use of her if not –* 'Do you understand?'

Miss Lottie Williams-Parry remained standing in the same position for some time. For a moment, waiting for a response from her, it seemed to Cecil there was a stillness. He became conscious of the river chuckling to itself as it twisted its way through the valley below, indifferent to the recent savagery in the lane. Somewhere over the fields he heard a dog bark and the cawing of the rooks on the other side of the cemetery.

She was unmoving except for her eyes blinking and sweeping over the scene. He asked her again in Welsh. With a start she seemed to come to, slipping her wallet into her shoulder bag. 'Dispose of them, you mean. Well there's two new graves in the cemetery just been dug but they're spoken for, you see.'

He looked across the valley. An idea came to him. 'How about the lead mine?'

'Yes. It's a Heritage Centre now.'

'And the mine shaft?'

'It's got a grill on top. Padlocked, isn't it? But there's the airshaft up on the mountain. It's not part of the Centre.'

'I remember it from way back. There's a track. I should be able get to it with this car. Will there be anyone about?'

'No, not a soul. Nobody ever goes up there now but I expect that shaft will be covered and padlocked too.'

He patted his pistol. 'It won't be a problem. Will you give me a hand?'

'I might as well.' Inconsistent with the circumstances, though it may have been nervous shock, she smiled, adding, 'I've got nothing else to do right now.'

79

Chapter Twenty-Two

Cecil went round to the man in the driving seat. He was slumped half out of the car, spilling blood and brains on the road. For a moment, a knot of dense bitter and burning liquid began to form in his stomach. It started to rise in his throat, bringing tears to his eyes, before he had it under control. He had a moment of anxiety in case it would be a sight too much for Miss Lottie Williams-Parry but it just prompted a muttered '*Ych a fi*' from her. A sticker on the dashboard told him the car was hired from a London company. Together they bundled the driver into the back. Picking up the Makarov and replacing it in his waistband holster, Cecil clipped it in his belt, grabbed the keys, and looked in the boot. Finding a blanket, he started to mop up as much of the blood as possible from the road on both sides of the car but gave up, throwing it back into the boot. Then they went to the body on the other side and lifted it into the back, Cecil tossed in the pistol and his bag. 'OK, get in,' he said. 'You can direct me from here.'

Crossing the river by the bridge, he drove up the old track until the low stone wall surrounding the air shaft came into view. Pulling over onto the sheep-cropped turf, he switched off the engine. As if by silent agreement, they sat still for some moments, hearing nothing except the wind rocking the car and the faint bleating of sheep. Suddenly he got out, followed quickly by Miss Lottie Williams-Parry, as if she didn't relish the idea of sitting in the car with two corpses.

Looking around over the rolling heather of the moorland there wasn't a sign of humanity to be seen, except down below in the village, where the muted sound of traffic drifted up. He went over to examine the hinged iron grating closing the shaft. It was secured by a bolt and a heavy padlock encrusted with rust. Ferns grew from inside the shaft wall, coiling their tips around the grating as if seeking to wrench a way to sunlight and freedom. Picking up a sizable stone, he reached over and dropped it through the bars giving a grunt of approval when it took some seconds for the watery 'splash' to reverberate up from the depths. Tearing some clumps of turf from around the shaft, he stacked them over the lock, weighing them down with a flat stone. 'Stand back,' he ordered. Drawing the pistol, he poked the muzzle into the turves and fired. A muffled thump echoed and re-echoed down the shaft. Clearing the smoking clumps, they could see the lock had disintegrated, leaving the bolt free to be drawn. After that, he was thankful for Miss Lottie Williams-Parry's hefty build as the two of them heaved open the weighty ironwork.

Dragging the corpses out of the car one by one, they tipped them over the stone wall to plummet head first down into the blackness. They were followed by their pistols. Once again they heaved the grating over to drop shut with a clang.

'Now I need to get rid of this car,' he said. 'Someone's bound to draw the attention of the police to a blood-drenched vehicle.'

Miss Lottie Williams-Parry grimaced with disgust.

'Where do the local joyriders go to torch theirs?'

She directed him down a lane leading to a rocky outcrop he remembered from long ago, about a mile below the village in the valley of the River Dee. It had become a fly-tippers' paradise.

Grabbing his bag, he got out of the car. At once, he was confronted by the hazy silhouette of the Pontcysyllte Aqueduct, spanning the deep valley thirty-eight metres above the river, bringing back memories. The sun in the south slipped from behind the clouds and the play of light picked out the detail of the iron arched ribs carrying the canal trough on masonry pillars. The water in the trough was less than a metre deep. It was more than enough for the narrow boat he spotted as it seemed to float through the sky on its traverse.

He and the other boys are late for school. They can hear the bell but playing on the towpath mounted over the canal is far too absorbing for it to have any meaning. The widely spaced eighteenth century railings of crude wrought iron bars are close enough to protect a horse from a terrible plunge but not a careless fully grown adult walking along a towpath barely wide enough for two people side by side. The other side of the trough has nothing between the boatmen and the dizzying drop. Now they are daring Huw to do his stunt again. He slips easily between the thick bars of the railings and holding on to them he leans out over the river and passes along the outside of the path, bar by slippery smooth bar, until he reaches the highest point before clambering back. And then they are swimming under the towpath, exploring the underworld of iron lattice-work that supports it.

Neither Cecil nor Lottie had matches nor a lighter so, not wanting to use up too much ammunition, he picked up a length of old pipe from the rubbish dump and spiked the fuel tank a few times. Taking a mat from the car he soaked part of it in the growing pool of petrol. Making sure they both stood well back he fired one round from the Makarov into the saturated part of the mat, igniting it from the muzzle flash before tossing it under the tank.

There was a satisfying 'whump' and a ball of flame enveloped the vehicle. Then they walked back up to the village with Cecil clutching his holdall. Somehow it had come to seem important to him, as if it was a kind of talisman, perhaps. Thick dark smoke was billowing up behind them when Miss Lottie Williams-Parry asked him, 'Well, what are you going to do now?'

It was indeed a question that had been exercising Cecil since she first appeared at the scene of his abduction. *She could be useful as a way of staying under cover in the village*, he thought. *She thinks I'm still part of the legitimate operation but stringing her along to keep her from reporting to Hackett can only be for so long. Somehow I'll have to win her over as* my *asset and not Hackett's.*

He said, 'I need somewhere to rest up for a while before I contact Control. Somewhere in the village.'

'You could come to my house.'

'Your house?'

'There's just me.'

'Just you – what about neighbours and people around? What would they make of a strange man appearing? The whole village would know about me within the hour.'

'Oh, it's not as bad as that these days, you know. Most of my neighbours are from away. I don't have anything to do with them.'

Chapter Twenty-Three

Miss Lottie Williams-Parry's house was one of a row of respectable detached villas in the lower part of the village.

Built of dressed stone at the turn of the last century, they fronted the main road going east down the hill. Bushes of broom amid larch trees faced the houses from across the road. Stunted by the prevailing wind, they clung stubbornly to the looming spoil bank of a derelict colliery. Cecil followed her up a short drive, more weeds than gravel, passing a dull grey Vauxhall Vectra at least ten years old. There was a side gate, he noted, probably opening onto a path leading to the rear of the house.

As they entered the hall, his trained senses were alert. Experience had taught him much could be learned about a person from the interior of their home. Their history is usually revealed by the place in which they have lived for any length of time. In the hall, there was a staircase of dark brown carpentry with brass stair rods, tarnished and dull, securing an elderly carpet. There appeared to be three doors off the L-shaped passage, so he assumed there was probably at least one more around the corner. The first door was unlatched. He stopped, letting her walk on, and eased it open, peering into what was the front room to check it out. Thin yellow curtains drawn across the windows gave a sulphurous light to the plain walls and to the room itself. Near the windows was a grand piano. The gold lettering of the name *Blüthner* was the only flash of colour in the room. The lid was open and there were dog-eared sheets of music on the stand, slumped to one side as if exhausted at standing in the same position for some time. He was drawn into the room to look more closely at two sepia photographs in silver frames on the marble mantle, flanking a clock in an onyx case. One was of a woman with a severe hairstyle and a tight-necked blouse with her lips pursed as if she was carrying out an unpleasant task. The other was of a man with a full moustache and unruly hair, despite being combed for the benefit of the camera. His chin was held up above his clerical collar as if he was about to deliver a sermon. The hands of the clock were stopped. One wall was entirely given over to books. He took out his spectacles holding the wire frames to his eyes with one hand as he perused the faded titles on tattered spines. The floor was of uncarpeted wood blocks. There was nothing else in the room but for a chair at a small table in a corner, facing a wall covered with framed certificates and faded diplomas. The table was empty except for a brass desk light with a green shade. The surfaces held a fine grey dust that clung to his fingers.

He followed her through the second door that led into a living room at the rear of the house. Looking through the window, he saw a neglected kitchen garden bounded by a high stone wall. There was a fireplace with an unlit gas fire. Books and sheets of music were piled on a bench in front of the window. In the middle of the room was a dining table accompanied by a suite of four chairs. One was drawn out, facing a laptop with papers scattered around it. The others were pushed under, as if they hadn't been used for a long time. By the fireplace were two threadbare easy chairs with shabby cushions. Some books lay around them on the worn carpet.

He stood at the window. 'What's beyond that wall at the end of the garden?'

'Fields, just fields.' She was in the doorway of what he took to be the kitchen. He could see there was an outer door opening onto a brick paved yard.

'Houses?'

'Not until you get to Rhos, three miles away.'

'The car's yours, I take it?'

'Yes.'

'Does it run?'

'It did last week.'

'Why didn't you go to the cemetery in it today?'

'I prefer to walk up there.' She coloured a little, lowering her gaze.

'Exercise?'

She nodded with her head still lowered.

'You have a mobile phone?'

She looked up. 'Yes.'

He acknowledged this information with a grunt and a curt shrug, followed by some moments with both of them looking at each other in awkward silence before she broke it. 'Would you like something to eat?'

He nodded and she disappeared into the kitchen where he heard her opening a tin and immediately his senses were overwhelmed by the smell of soup or stew of some sort becoming more intense as it heated up in a microwave oven. He realised how desperately hungry he was. Presently she brought a stack of sliced bread onto the table and went back for two steaming bowls. He pulled out a chair while she did the same and he gave his attention completely to the hot stew, attacking it ravenously. Suddenly a wave of exhaustion seemed to close in on him. His eyelids were becoming too heavy to keep open, even as he was mopping up the stew with the bread. The events of the last twenty-four hours were taking their toll. His head started to nod.

'You need to lie down for a while.' Her voice roused him. 'Go up to the front bedroom.'

He didn't need persuading. As he climbed the stairs, he comforted himself with the thought that talking her round could keep until later. Nevertheless, he had impressed on her that attempting to use her contact numbers was not to be done. He would speak to her later about it after he'd had a brief rest.

When he reached the landing he glanced in the back bedroom, just to be on the safe side. It was clear and curiously bare of furniture. Not even a bed. Somehow he knew the spare bedroom would be the same. He was right. The woman had offered him her only bed. Well, he'd just take a short rest, two hours or so. Exhausted, he threw his jacket over a chair, eased out the Makarov and took off the shoulder holster with the Glock. He pushed them under a pillow. The last thing he remembered was kicking off his shoes and lying down on top of the large double bed without disturbing the bedclothes.

Chapter Twenty-Four

At first he became aware of a white horizontal strip gradually becoming yellow and then golden. It had been there for some time before he realised it was the sun coming through the gap between the bottom of the curtains and the windowsill. As the dimness of the room gave way to a clearer light he began to take in his surroundings. He could make out a basketwork chair with his jacket thrown on it. There was a monumental mahogany wardrobe and a dressing table to match. Its top was completely bare, prompting a feeling of emptiness that seemed to envelope him. The house itself seemed empty – empty of the scents of polish, of flowers, of the sounds of a clock, of the impact on the eye of ornaments. It was an emptiness that lay upon the house like a cold mantle. It provoked the feeling of bleak almost melancholic sadness he had experienced on first crossing the threshold.

With a start, he sat up, wide awake. Bedclothes fell away, confusing him. How did they come to be here? *They must have been drawn over me while I was asleep.* Checking under the pillows, he retrieved the pistols and, looking at his watch, he tried and failed to make sense of the time. There was an acrid cindery smell of burnt toast. *A sign of life downstairs,* he thought. As he drew the curtains, a blaze of sunlight exploded into the room, rendering him sightless for a few seconds so that he stumbled over his holdall bag at the foot of the bed.

After he'd washed and shaved in the cold water of the austere bathroom, he decided to keep wearing the shabby clothes. As he wasn't sure he would be staying, he went down, taking his bag with him.

Miss Lottie Williams-Parry was standing at a table laboriously stirring a pan of what looked to be a dense porridge recently heated in the microwave oven. '*Bore da*,' she greeted him. 'I didn't have much luck with the toast,' she added cheerfully. 'Not much good at cooking, see, so I threw it out for the birds. I—'

Cutting across her, he asked, 'Where did you sleep?'

'Oh, I decided not to disturb you. Out cold, you were. You must have needed it, so I just pulled the covers over. I slept there,' she nodded to the easy chair. 'I often do that when I can't be bothered going upstairs.'

The porridge was reluctant to leave the pan. He watched her as she fought to spoon it into two bowls. Salt was sprinkled on it and the bowls were set down on the table. After they'd breakfasted, with the things washed up, they sat in the easy chairs drinking tea. During the grim and silent struggle to eat the porridge, Cecil had assessed her state of mind. It confirmed his decision to attempt to use her and her home as a safe house. The car would be useful as well. *She seems amenable to an approach to bring her over. It worked well for me in the old days in Berlin but first I'll get her to tell her story. There's something poignant about this house. It should give me a chance to engage her feelings before I make my move.*

And so, when they finished their tea, he persuaded Lottie to begin her story.

'My parents had me late in life. I was born in this house and grew up in the village. Mam was a teacher in the local infants' school. It was the same school I attended. She gave singing lessons in the house. Dad was a deacon in the chapel. Fiercely Welsh, he was. He loved the Welsh language and put it across as a poet. He was quite well known for it, actually, but most of all he was known around here for his preaching. He believed that modern things in the home, you know, the vacuum cleaner and the television, turned people away from needs of the spirit and he allowed no place for them under this roof – not even a telephone. I still don't have one. I don't need one really. I use my mobile. But we had a gramophone. He liked that. There's still piles of old records somewhere.'

She cast her eyes around the room as if seeking them among the clutter. Turning back to Cecil she said, 'You know, growing up as an only child I never realised just how much my life was . . .' she struggled for the words for a moment, 'inward-looking, like, until I was eleven. At home it was piano practice, recitation, and singing. It was clear early on I had a good voice, even to me. At chapel and school it was concerts and the eisteddfod. Two evenings a week, I went up to the top of the village for lessons at my piano teacher's house.' She stopped. It was a part of her life she never talked about, not even to herself. As if she had no language to do so. Nevertheless it often flashed through her mind, catching her unawares and unsettling her.

Intrigued, Cecil broke into her reverie bringing her back to the present. 'What happened when you were eleven?'

'Well, I went to the grammar school down in the town. It had quite an effect on me, I can tell you. This was the first time I had been down to town, you see, and the first time I had been on a bus, too. Getting one to school each day, I was. The school seemed enormous but I soon learned its ways.' She slipped back again. The images flashed up but she shook herself mentally and went on. 'When I was eighteen I left home for Bangor University, School of Music. Eventually it led to an audition with Welsh National Opera at Cardiff,' she hesitated saying shyly, 'and I had an offer to join the company.'

Lottie fell silent again, as if that was the end of her story.

Cecil prompted her, 'So you took it up. And it led to a career?'

She shook her head.

He gave her a questioning look, affecting puzzlement in order to draw her out. *It must have been something out of the ordinary,* he thought, *to have stopped her on the threshold of her career and changed the course of her life as it so obviously had.*

'I turned it down.'

'You turned it down! Why?'

Lottie shrugged and looked away. 'Something happened.'

Cecil's senses quickened. Here's a chance to latch on to her emotions. To get through to her. This was the turning point that had worked so well in the past. 'What happened, Lottie?' He used her first name intentionally to prod her.

'Something happened – and I never took it up.' She gave a weak smile. 'I declined, you see. For thirty years I've got by at home with the teaching and the little bit of family money. There were the performances, concerts, and competitions of course but . . .' she sighed, 'over the last five years or so it's all dwindled. So I got the part-time position with the library in the village. That helps.' She stood up and went to stand in the window looking out, watched by Cecil. She turned back to him. 'I don't know where the time's gone, really.' She fell quiet again, then went back to her chair and sat down.

Cecil maintained an interrogator's silence, provoking the compulsion to break it.

Looking at the carpet, she spoke. 'Normally I don't give things much thought but when I look back over the last few years my life seems over – all in the past, like. I try to put things together, to make sense of things, but . . .' She looked up and, with a lift of her shoulders, her voice became stronger and higher pitched. 'Well, just now things seem to have taken me by the scruff of the neck and given me a good shaking.' She looked at Cecil, 'Never in my wildest dreams did I imagine what I've seen over the last few days nor what I've done either. Somehow the world seems a different kind of place now.'

Cecil leaned over to her and took her hand ready to press home his advantage. She didn't resist. 'Lottie, tell me what happened. How did you come to live your life in this place?' He glanced around the room. 'This place where things seems to have stood still. The books, the photos, and the rooms upstairs – everything so empty. Why?'

Should I tell him? Tell him what's going on within myself, she thought. *What's been going on for all these years since college so that I can't remember a time without it? This is a part of myself I've told no one about. Something not to be trusted with anyone else.*

She withdrew her hand.

91

And why him? To unpack these images before him, the dreams evoking the feelings, the deep sense of failure, of blame, of remorse, of shame. Should I tell him? I don't know. And who are these people anyway coming into my life like this, with their guns and dreadful violence? Suddenly the shattering window flashed before her. Once again she saw the vicious ferocity unleashed, the three slumped figures, the smashed heads, the blood and brains: shocking and appalling. Her eyes conveyed the contents of the room in sharp focus. She became aware of her heart fluttering and her limbs trembling. Her breath was coming in quick short gasps. Attempting to grasp the arms of the chair with shaking hands, she gave up and slumped back with a distinct feeling of detachment as if she was floating and looking down on herself.

Chapter Twenty-Five

'Lottie!' Cecil was gently slapping her face. As she slowly became conscious of her surroundings she felt a deep thirst.

As if he could feel it himself, Cecil said, 'I'll get you some tea.'

She nodded and he went into the kitchen. Lying back in the chair, she heard fumbling among the tins then the sound of the kettle and the fridge door sighing shut before he reappeared with a steaming mug. As she took it from him their hands touched. For a moment neither withdrew. A fleeting uncertainty struck him. Despite himself he let his hand dwell for some moments clasping hers a little before letting go.

'I don't know whether you take sugar but I've put plenty in. Drink it up anyway. You need it. Do you understand?'

She nodded again.

He watched her as she tasted it. It was hot. 'You've had a reaction to what you've seen and done over the last few days. Do you understand what I'm saying?'

She nodded again. 'Yes, I think so.'

'It might come back, especially when you're asleep, but it should only be for a brief spell. It will pass eventually. It affects all of us like that sooner or later.' He looked at her as she sipped the tea, calm but still shaken.

This onset of shock is convenient. It's come at just the right time, he thought as he sat down. Now he was ready for the next stage. *I won't push it. I'll let her speak first.*

She put the mug down on the floor and looked up at him. 'You said it affects all of us sooner or later. What about you? Has it affected you?'

'Not for some time.'

'But it *has* affected you. When? Long ago . . . Lately?'

'Some years ago.'

'And you got over it, did you?'

'More or less.'

'More or less, was it?'

'Rarely now.' He shrugged. 'There are times . . .' He checked himself and left it unsaid. *This is going off track. On the other hand, perhaps I could use it to gain some sympathy.* 'Things went wrong,' he continued. 'It was difficult. So difficult it left me with unpleasant episodes. Not unlike yours, but much worse.' *I'll have to go carefully here. I've not talked about it to anyone before.*

'What happened then?'

As if the dam was broken, he found himself telling her about the cell, the darkness, the slimy brick walls, the damp floor, the overflowing slops, prisoners coughing, spitting, murmuring of voices, gurgling of pipes, screams, and the constant fear. And above all the interrogation, the water, the terror. Afterwards the dreams of drowning and suffocation that still follow and the vivid recurring memories stalking him, lying in wait to strike at a moment of weakness. So vivid that he daren't take a shower nor lift his face to falling rain.

When he finished, there was a deep silence. What had he done? He felt vulnerable and exposed, but perhaps now was the time to exploit the situation. 'So I know how you felt just now.'

Lottie was silent for some time. He let her sit quietly until she spoke. 'Mr Syssel?'

'Yes.'

'Huw Syssel, isn't it?'

'It is, Lottie. You can call me Huw.'

'When are you going to get in touch with our colleagues?'

This is it. Now's the time to tell her. It'll be a hell of a risk but it's worth a longshot. After all, what choice do I have? If it doesn't work, I'll have to deal with her. Here goes. 'I'm not going to get in touch with them, Lottie.'

There was a tense pause. 'You're not going to get in touch with them.' It was a bald statement delivered in a flat voice.

He shook his head.

For a brief moment it seemed to Cecil that his heartbeat slowed almost to a stop as he waited to see how she would take it.

Lottie stirred in her chair. 'I only helped you because I thought we were on the same side, sort of both in it together, like.' She paused before going on. 'You know, I had a feeling something was not right. You've made no mention of them at all, despite what's gone on since yesterday.' *He's exploited me, abused my trust. Not again surely, I'm not being used again.* Her forehead flushed, becoming almost the colour as her hair. The freckles around her nose deepened and her breathing laboured. Surprised by the welling of anger pent up from the past, she fought to control herself but it was in vain. Seizing the mug from the floor she sprang up and hurled it at him in an explosion of wrath, giving out a great scream of fury. Cecil just had time to dodge as it passed his head, shattering on the wall behind him in a dramatic explosion leaving runnels of tea. Lottie collapsed back in her chair trembling and still breathing deeply.

He waited until her breathing steadied before he spoke. 'Look, I didn't choose to meet you in that lane any more than you chose to meet me. It was you who offered me this house as shelter, remember? We've been thrown together.' As she calmed, he spoke: he started with the Berlin Friendship House and the compromising material, but only hinting without going into detail. Then he spoke about Hackett's mission to capture it and hand it over to the authorities for elimination. He followed that with the attempt on his life and about Voronov, describing the events at the bog. Finally he told her how he came to be in the village and how he intended to get the material, which he explained was on microfilm, out in the public domain.

Throughout his account, Lottie remained still, staring intently at Cecil, her hands gripping the arms of her chair.

'So you see, that's why I need a safe house for now. Somewhere to wait out Hackett's next move before I get back into Llangollen and sniff out the microfilm. I was planning on taking a room for a few days somewhere in the village but those SVR goons jumped me.' After he concluded his rushed story, he waited expectantly for a response.

This is a chancy situation, Lottie thought. Her anger was dissipating in the face of rising anxiety. *Even more so than it seemed at first. He wants to hide in this house, hide from the people who drew me into this mess. What if I refuse to help and report him? What if he thinks I might report him? It's clear from what I've seen that he's a dangerous man, awfully dangerous.* She felt beads of cold sweat break out on her forehead. *And if I help him, if I don't tell them about him, I set myself against them as well.*

Cecil felt the need to break into her thoughts. 'That's where you came in, and saved my life. It's time I thanked you.'

She ignored him for a moment. *I'll keep him talking. Yes, that's it. I'll try and find out why he's so set on exposing the material on that microfilm.* 'Why are you telling me this? You could have stayed here for a few days before leaving to get on with your business without dragging me into it. Come to think of it, you could still do that. All I have to do is nothing. You go off in a couple of days and that's it.' Despite her fear, she surprised herself once again as she expressed a flash of still smouldering fury. 'Just don't mention me to this Hackett man. And anyway, what's so important about what happened at that place? Politicians and corruption: it happens all the time. Why not let them do what they like with that film? All those people dead – for what?'

Cecil shrugged mentally. *There's nothing for it but to tell her what's on the microfilm.*

And so he told her.

He told her how, during the Cold War, the house was set up by the KGB in the Soviet sector of East Berlin. Firstly as a honey trap for diplomats, civil servants, lawyers and judges visiting from the West. But by the eighties it was functioning with the specific purpose of catering for the paedophilic tastes of certain high-ranking politicians particularly from the UK establishment. He named some of them, causing Lottie to gasp in astonishment.

Cecil went on to tell about the young boys and the thirteen-year-old girls brought over from the orphanages in Eastern Europe. Some were kidnapped off the streets. Many were murdered and all of it was provided for the pleasure of the clients and graphically recorded in the closest detail for the KGB files.

Lottie was shaken by what she was hearing. *I thought such things had only happened to me*, she thought. *To find out others have been through it and experienced the same feelings, the same assault on their being – oh God, I'm not the only one.*

'Since the beginning of the nineties,' he went on, 'the Berlin Friendship House was thought to have disappeared into the dustbin of history including the material the KGB had on file. But it re-emerged on microfilm in the hands of Voronov and all concerned want to get hold of it, including me. As I told you earlier, Hackett is my case officer and, although you haven't met him, he knows all about you. He's ruthlessly ambitious and obsessed with his mission to obtain that film for his masters by whatever means necessary—'

'Children from orphanages.' Lottie's voice broke in as if she hadn't been listening. It was flat, almost expressionless, 'thirteen-year-old schoolgirls?'

'That's right. Thousands of them, little girls and boys. All of it filmed by the latest technology of the day. Everyone taking part is identifiable and most of them are still alive. What a coup for the KGB, don't you think? Except it was never used.'

'Never used? Why not?'

Cecil shrugged. 'Deals were done, I suppose. We'll never know the answer. But now both sides are after it. One side to use it as blackmail, as was intended in the first place, one side to destroy it and shield the people in it. And I want to get it out before the public so those . . . those *creatures* can be shown up for what they are and be held to account. I tried before, almost had the stuff in my hands, but I found out what the authorities were going to do with it and I let it go. I'm not going to let this second chance slip away. Perhaps I can stop this sort of thing from happening again but I need to find some way of getting it onto a disk or something so it can be put out.'

'So why should I believe this is true?' She found Cecil's story hardly credible and yet it stirred something in her mind, something she knew only too well. *The use of those children, those young people, their feelings, what they must have gone through, what many of them must still be going through.*

Cecil raised an eyebrow, 'Why else should I risk my neck? When you stumbled on me yesterday, you saved my life but you put yours on the line. If Hackett makes the connection between you and me, you're in big trouble. He's not working to defend the realm. Oh no. His role is to protect those people in high places who are implicated in that dreadful business that went on in East Berlin all those years ago. His brief is to use whatever means necessary and always in secret so we're cut off from access to the institutions of the state, the police, the judiciary and such. And they from us. We're on our own.'

Cecil's voice seemed distant. She could hear what he was saying but it seemed to belong elsewhere. His story had set off those dreadful feelings. She felt them boiling up. The pressure was almost unbearable. Her mind was in turmoil.

'Think about what happened, Lottie. Surely you can imagine what it was like for them at the time and afterwards. For the rest of their lives they—'

'Yes!' she screamed.

Cecil recoiled.

Holding back sobs, she said quietly, 'Yes I know. I know what it was like.'

Cecil made to continue speaking but she held up her hand as if to stay him. *Should I tell him all?* The question was redundant. The die was already cast. The need for release from the burden of the past was overwhelming.

First she told him about the piano teacher. It was still difficult to find the language to express the feelings in words but they came out with a lucidity of their own. 'A respected member of the chapel, he was. Living alone since his mother died some years before. It started at the piano lessons soon after the beginning of the grammar school. The touching and the fumbling was tentative at first. I would sit rigid. I couldn't understand what was going on. He took it as compliance, I suppose. As if I was going along with it. Then it became persistent, forceful, intrusive and all the time without anything being said. Blanketed in secrecy, it became an intimate part of the lessons. The disgust; the revulsion; the shame at allowing it to happen; the guilt at somehow causing it, somehow causing a highly respected man to do such things.'

These feelings were locked deep in Lottie, and with time they had grown into a smouldering fury that she should be so burdened with them.

Cecil listened without speaking. Though each sentence was confirming to him the effectiveness of his plan to get her to tell her story he was becoming aware of inconvenient feelings being engendered.

She told him about college. 'I never had any real friends at college. Kept myself to myself, you know, wasn't much of a mixer, see, just kept my head down. I didn't even join any clubs or groups. It was in my final year when it started. In his forties, he was. A singing teacher – not mine, though – on the staff at the college. I'd not taken much notice of him 'til then. Never gave him much thought. I didn't think he would have anything to do with someone like me anyway. We got talking over coffee one day.' She reflected, 'John Morgan, he was. Married, no children. Ruth, his wife's name was. She was attractive. They lived in a house near the college. It was a cold marriage, he said, in name only – I believed him. I just took it for granted. If I could see a future in it at all, I suppose I thought – well, eventually he would leave her. The marriage would end mutually and our relationship – what we had – would just go on.' She smiled as if inwardly recalling it. 'I was flattered. God, yes, I was flattered. We used to meet in the week, one or two evenings, for a drink and sandwiches. Then we'd go back to my room at college. He would sneak away in the early hours. It all seemed so romantic and exciting, not a bit nasty, as I came to see it later. Often at weekends, Saturdays and Sundays, he would take a room over a pub in Red Wharf Bay, a few miles away on Anglesey. They knew him there, you see. It overlooked the beach where we sometimes had picnics . . .' Lottie turned in her chair and looked out of the window with vacant eyes. Unbidden, the image of his lean sunburnt frame entered her mind and faded. 'It turned out it was a game for him.' There was a bitter edge to her voice. 'He had others. His wife was in on it. She didn't mind. It seemed I was one of many. She said it helped to strengthen the marriage.'

Lottie turned from the window. 'I can remember getting the offer from Welsh National Opera as if it was yesterday. It was the day before my twenty-first birthday, 1987.' She recalled the moment as she looked into the middle distance somewhere over Cecil's shoulder. 'Oh, what a joy it was. Oh, such a feeling.' With a start, as if reluctant to let it go, she went on, 'I decided not to tell Mam and Dad until I went home the following week for the Easter recess. I could just picture how delighted they would be. Dad standing there so proud like, and Mam would be sitting holding the tips of her fingers together as she did when she was pleased.' She paused as if to enjoy the fleeting images. 'But I decided to tell John that evening and to book a table for us at our usual place. I'd say it was to celebrate my birthday.' She heaved a sigh. 'Well, you see, I'd phone him daily at his room in college. That's if he didn't call me first. It was part of what we had, part of the relationship. I knew what time he was there on his own and we would talk about all sorts of things – I rang many times. There was no answer. The question rose in me like a chill mountain mist: why hadn't he rung me, not even at his usual time? I began to have a niggling nervousness in the pit of my stomach. I went a day like that and into the next. After a night without sleep I waited until late afternoon. I couldn't bear it any longer, see. I decided to ring his home. It was not supposed to be part of our arrangement. I thought, if his wife answered, I'd think of something to say. You know, like, some reason for phoning.'

Lottie paused as if gathering her thoughts. Her eyes seemed dull and inward looking. There were faint beads of perspiration along her upper lip.

'It rang once, twice, three times . . . and on the fourth he picked it up. "Yes?" he said. Just like that, "Yes?"'

'"It's me," I said, feeling sheepish, "Lottie. I've been calling you." "I know," he said. The coldness in his voice set me back so that my heart seemed to stop. "I can't talk right now," he said. "I'll call you later." There was a click and the call ended.'

Lottie leaned forward in her chair. 'I can't remember deciding to go to his house but there I was on the doorstep. He looked surprised, startled even. I was puzzled. Not believing what my mind was telling me, you see. I decided to ignore the rising dread inside me and go on as if nothing was wrong. So I made my suggestion of a celebration meal. It must have sounded awfully limp. He said he couldn't come out that evening.

'"What do you mean?" I asked. I couldn't believe what I was hearing. He'd arranged to go out for dinner with someone else – his wife.'

She took a deep breath before going on. 'I must have protested in some way, though looking back, the only thing I can remember is my world crumbling while over it all I could hear was him calmly explaining the situation. If I couldn't accept the state of affairs, maybe it was time to end things. He set out how he saw it. Surely I could understand that. What did I think was going to happen? It was all fun while it lasted, wasn't it? I was young enough to look back on it as a pleasant experience, a bit of excitement . . .

'I can remember shouting, "What about your wife? Would she see it as a *bit of excitement?*" Then I heard, "As a matter of fact I do." His wife had come out to the hall at that moment. "You're one of his peccadilloes, my dear." Yes that was the word, *peccadillo*. "It's a failing he has and I indulge him," she said. Well, I turned to him. He just put his head down and walked away down the hall, leaving her standing there with her arms folded. The last I remember as I went down the steps was feeling her staring into my back.'

Chapter Twenty-Six

Lottie stood up and walked over to the window. As she passed Cecil he touched her arm. It was a tender gesture done without thinking and he saw the flush of warmth creep up her neck. She spoke to the window. Her voice was flat. 'I never told Mam and Dad why I came home before the end of term and never went back. They never asked. I suppose they thought college was too much for me. Nor did I tell them about the offer from Welsh National Opera.' She turned her head from the window, looking back at Cecil. 'I just couldn't do it, see. In fact, I couldn't do anything. My memory of that time is fogged even now. I must have been a great trial to them. Me just sitting around, mostly in my bedroom.'

Brightening up, she turned to him. 'Do you know this is the first time I've talked about it? I mean, looked back on purpose, brought it all out and unpacked it, like. Not just when those times sneak into my mind, when I'm caught off guard. It's not what I want to do but somehow, since what has happened over the last few days, I feel the need to dig into the blackness and pull things out. All I can recall are feelings: humiliation; remorse; guilt; and such shame, such *deep* shame. I felt that somehow I must have deserved to be treated in that way.' Then she went over to her chair and sat down with her hands in her lap looking at Cecil. 'But I can put a name to those feelings now. It's as if I've drawn them out into the open, caught them in a box and thrown it away.'

Her mood changed again as if the past was weighing too heavily for her to cast it off. 'Sometimes I couldn't decide whether or not to get up, or what clothes to put on if I did. As for my music – well, I couldn't read nor sing a note, nor did I want to. I never looked at the piano at all. Time would mean nothing. I'd sit down with my mind a blank and come to finding hours had gone by. And food, it meant nothing to me. I became so thin, believe it or not, loose skin was hanging off me. I remember being aware of how I looked. I would go to great lengths to keep away from people who knew me, the milkman, and the postman, even Mam and Dad. I couldn't bear the look on their faces, you see. Those looks were shocking. They made me curl up inside. They thought I was ill. I suppose I was, in a way, but a doctor was out of the question. I think they sensed that. It was never mentioned. Going out was torture. The village streets were frightening places. I couldn't bear to respond to anyone.'

Cecil sat unmoving, watching her. He hadn't expected things to go so deep and he didn't know how to respond, how to stop his feelings being engaged.

'Dad died a year later. In a way, I felt a release rather than a loss – in fact, I had no feelings for him nor for Mam. He was no longer there to be my judge, see. His presence had been a force of blame hanging over me.'

She sat in silence for some moments, lost in thought. Cecil suppressed an urge to prompt her.

She went on, 'It was some time before I realised the darkness was lifting. Just before Mam went into decline and died. Pneumonia it was. Both of them were gone without knowing why I came home or about the offer from Welsh National Opera. Nothing was ever said. I can't remember speaking to them at all during that time. Gradually, bit by bit, I started to come around, though I never got over it. I still haven't got over it, even after all these years. I think having to go to the shops did it. You know? Got me out. It was that or starve. My appetite came back, you see. It forced me to speak to people. I can't remember how, but I joined a choir in the village and things went from there. Someone suggested I went for the part-time post in the village library. That led to the teaching – the piano – the singing. I threw myself into it, I suppose. I became quite a celebrity in the County. *The* Miss Lottie Williams-Parry, the person I am known as today – not the one who went to college.' She gave a wistful smile, 'The person who could have been.' Then she sighed. 'But time passes.'

'And after college, has there been no one since?'

Lottie looked down and shook her head. 'I could never respond to – you know,' she faltered awkwardly, 'that sort of thing. For years, I could barely bring myself to speak to a man, under any circumstances.'

'You're managing all right now,' Cecil found himself saying. He watched her acutely as she seemed to him to come alive, losing her flabby presence. For the first time her eyes appeared bright blue to him, no longer dull and lifeless.

'Yes I am, aren't I? Do you know, when I think back over what's happened these last few days, what I've seen, and what I've done, I don't recognise myself. Was that me, really me?' She looked reflectively at her hands for some seconds before looking up again. 'And you, the man who has his name and address on a gravestone, how have you come to be the man you are?'

Unexpectedly, Cecil felt uneasy as he became conscious of wanting to respond to her. It was not as a way of bringing her over, but because he wanted to tell her what he'd discovered and to tell her about *his* feelings. Unconsciously he was losing his cynicism, dropping his guard. Also he wanted to tell her how he felt cheated, used as a substitute, and how the life he thought he had lived was a sham. A life that was a charade acted out for the benefit of others. As he told her, he became aware again of how desperate he was to discover his real identity.

When he finished they both sat for some moments until she broke the silence, 'Do you have a wife, children?'

'When I first met my wife she was living in the house where she grew up. It was left her by her parents, a large one in a Georgian terrace. It's on Mall Road, near Hammersmith Bridge. It became our home after we were married.'

He paused to gather his thoughts and to steady himself, realising it was the first time he'd talked about it. 'She died in 1986, killed by an IRA bomb, Christmas shopping in Harrods.' He gave a weak smile. 'A present for me. She was twenty-seven. We'd been married about eighteen months.' He paused. 'We never had children. I've lived in the house on my own ever since.' For the first time, it occurred to him there was not much difference between Lottie's house and his. Both stilled in time. Both empty of human warmth and purpose. 'I never seemed to find a reason to move and, since retiring, I decided to stop thinking about it. As you said, time passes.'

Where do we go from here? Do I throw in my lot with him? All of a sudden, Lottie understood what was happening to her. The situation offered a chance to make up for thirty lost years. Thirty years having missed out on fulfilment. Here was a chance to do something worthwhile.

Could she trust him? She wanted to trust him. 'You can stay here as long as you need!' she exclaimed. 'And I'll take my chances with this man Hackett.'

For a moment Cecil was taken aback. *Things are moving quicker than I expected. Perhaps I should act now in case she changes her mind.* 'He's not alone. He has great resources, all that the state can provide. Think on what I've just said. You have to be sure.' He thought, *why did I feel the need to say that? I've done it. I've brought her over. That's what I want, isn't it? All the same, am I sure why I'm putting her at such risk? Sure that it's not out of a sense of personal grievance? Those deaths: are they worth what I'm seeking to do or are they perhaps about revenge, about getting back at the Service? The Service I've served with such loyal devotion. The Service which now aims to destroy me? Is that how it is? Do I see things as they are? No matter. If it is out of personal grievance, the successful outcome will justify it anyway and putting her at risk is a price I'm willing to pay – isn't it?* He realised he wasn't sure.

Her voice broke into his thoughts, firm and certain. 'Yes, I'm sure.'

He looked at her. In his eyes it seemed she was changing, becoming steely and more assured, provoking feelings in him akin to admiration, even perhaps affection.

She asked, 'When you get the microfilm, what are you going to do with it?'

'Well I have this idea of putting it out online, you know, on social media, but to do that I have to get it transferred onto something. I don't know what it's called—'

'Digitising and scanning,' she interrupted.

'What?'

'Digitising and scanning. I often have to go down to the main library in town to transfer microfilmed documents onto disk or microfiche. I have to digitise them and then scan them onto a disk.'

'You could do that?'

'It shouldn't be a problem. There's no one looking over my shoulder when I use the equipment. It could even be put out on the internet from there.'

'Wonderful!' he exclaimed. 'We'll go into Llangollen this afternoon.'

'This afternoon? So soon? Are we ready?'

'As ready as we'll ever be.' He took out Voronov's card with the address of the walkers' hostel and held it up. There was a bloody thumbprint on it. 'I think this is where Voronov was staying but there's little chance the microfilm's there. It's just not his style. Anyway Hackett would have traced him to there and had his people all over the place by now, and they'll have left a number to call as soon as anyone makes enquiries.'

'So where is it then?'

'Well, I think I know, or at least where Voronov has left a clue.'

'What do you mean?'

'During the course of our conversation, I asked him how I would find the microfilm if something were to happen to him. He hinted that he had stashed it somewhere in the town.'

'And?'

'When he was dying, I got out of him the words, "the shop".

That's all, "the shop". I've been thinking about it on and off since. He used a newsagent's shop in the town as a drop-off box to contact me. It's standard practice. I'd already set it up and all he had to do was make a simple enquiry at each newsagent in the town. I doubt whether there's more than two or three. So, you see, I think he's left a message at that shop, as a form of insurance, I suppose, before he came to meet me. But the minute I'm in the open they'll have me under observation. Hackett will have eyes all over the town. However, although they will have taken the details of your car and phone when you were recruited, they have no reason yet to connect you to me. We have two advantages over them at present. One, they think I'm alone and on foot and, two, your appearance is still unknown to them. So this is what I want you to do: drive into town with me guiding you from the seat behind. Park as close to the door as possible. I get out and into the shop. When I come out, I dive into the back on the floor. You pull away in the traffic, making your way to the junction of the A5, turning east at the lights and driving out of the town. What we do next depends on what has happened in the shop.'

'Wait a minute,' Lottie interrupted, 'why don't you stay here and I go in to Llangollen to get it?'

'I fear it won't work. Voronov would have given my description as the man who came for the Russian paper and instructed that whatever it is it should be given to that person alone.'

'What if he's not left any message there?'

'Then that's the end of it,' he shrugged. 'The microfilm's lost for all time.'

There was a pause. Cecil walked over to the window and appeared to be looking out. Mentally he counted to ten. He turned back to her. 'Look, I still think it's worth a try. What do you think?'

'I think we should go for it.'

'You'll need a bag packed, nothing big, something the same size as mine. We may be away for some time.'

'I've got a small rucksack.'

'That will do. Bring your phone charger as well as your phone and we must make sure they're charged up. Before we go, I want you to track over the route until you know it by heart. And now I must ask you something important.' He paused. 'Are you sure you want to go through with this? It could get – well – dangerous.'

She nodded twice. 'Yes.'

'OK. Get your stuff together and let's go.'

Chapter Twenty-Seven

Lottie eased her car through the busy street, with Cecil crouching on the floor. It was crowded, shoppers and visitors overflowing the pavements and challenging the traffic. 'There's no room to park in front of the shop. What do I do now?' Her voice betrayed her anxiety.

'Go round again. If I'm out in the open a moment longer than necessary it's too much of a risk.'

'All right, but we should only try once more or we'll start to attract attention.' Panic was creeping up on her.

'OK. Calm down. You'll just have to drop me off and wait somewhere. When I'm ready to come out, I'll phone. You get there with all speed, as if your life depends on it, and be ready to head out east on the A5. Do you understand?'

'Yes.'

Cecil stepped cautiously out of the car. He looked up and down the street. It was a stream of faces and the backs of heads flowing both ways. *Hackett's men are here somewhere, and in twos probably*, he thought. Briskly as possible, he weaved through the eddying passers-by crossing the pavement and entered the quiet calm of the shop. It appeared to be empty of customers except for an elderly man. He reminded Cecil of an ancient tortoise as he stooped over his walking stick, stretching his long wrinkled neck as he furtively sifted through the top shelf of periodicals. Cecil approached the counter. A young woman looked up from browsing her iPhone with plump fingers and black varnished nails.

Without any initial opening, he blurted out, 'Has something been left for me in the name of Smith, Mr Smith?'

For a moment, her face was blank. 'Mr Roberts is not in today. He'll know. Can you come back tomorrow? He'll be here then.'

Cecil's heart sank. 'I'm afraid not. Can you get in touch with him now? It's urgent.'

There was a moment's hesitation, 'I tell you what: I'll phone him now on the landline. Will you keep an eye on things?' She eyed the old man meaningfully. 'It's in the back.'

Cecil nodded and, with a flounce, she disappeared behind a screen to leave him anxiously waiting at the counter. The ancient browser stopped leafing through a glossy man's magazine and eyed him curiously, making no attempt to communicate. Under his watchful gaze, Cecil pretended to peruse the shelves above the counter until, after what seemed an age, the woman breezed back into the shop and showed him a small sealed envelope. It was blank. Cecil felt disappointed and puzzled, expecting something more substantial. 'Is that all?'

She ignored the question. 'Mr Roberts said before I give it to you, I'm to ask you what newspaper you wanted when you came in before. It's just as a check, you know.'

'*Izvestiya.*'

'Here you are then.' She handed over the envelope. 'And Mr Roberts said "Do you still want the paper and, if not, will you pay up for the ones that we've ordered?" That will be six pounds and fifty pence.'

Cecil fumbled in his pocket for the money and handed it over. Going over to the newspaper stand, he took out his phone, aware that he was being watched all the time by both the woman and the old man. He keyed Lottie's number. Getting a reply, he uttered one word, 'Now.'

Looking through the glass door, he waited, counting the seconds as people passed back and to. Shortly the car pulled up in the line of traffic. Darting out and shuffling through the crowd, he snatched open the door as it pulled away and dived onto the floor in the back.

110

Chapter Twenty-Eight

'What kept you?' Lottie was irritated. 'I thought you were never going to call. Did you get it?'

'Never mind. Get this car onto the A5. It's left at the lights. I'll tell you what to do next.'

Lottie pushed the car out of the town as fast as the traffic would allow and, feeling safer, Cecil sat up in the back, keeping the rear view under scrutiny. 'You'll come to a sign for a golf club. It's a couple of miles on the left. Pull onto the drive; it will lead to a car park. That will do us.'

Lottie eased her car down the steep drive and parked up among the golfers' cars. 'What do we do now?'

'Now we sit here for a few minutes while I open this envelope.' He tore it open and cursed.

'What's wrong?'

'Nothing in it.' Overcoming the sudden wave of dismay, he noticed Cyrillic writing on the inside. Getting out of the car he read it. It was an address:

81 Broad Road, Tooting Broadway, SW17.

It was followed by a brief note:

Mrs Wilkinson. Package for Mr Smith. You will owe her £50.

He memorised it and, tearing the envelope into little pieces, he walked over to the boundary wall and threw them into the light breeze so that they were scattered over the adjoining field.

As he got back in the car, this time in the front beside Lottie, she asked what was in the note. 'I won't tell you. It's best you don't know. Not yet anyway.' Before she could object, he took a serious tone. 'Now I want you to drive back to your place and wait there.'

'But what about you?'

'I'm going to follow up on the information on the envelope. It'll take me some days, so don't try to contact me. When I come back, I expect to have the microfilm with me and then it will be up to you.'

'Why don't you take me with you?'

'It's safer if you go back to your house and wait there until I come back with the film. Things could get tricky where I'm going. There's no need for both of us to be in the frame together. As it is, they don't know you're in this with me. Your house is still a safe place for me to come back to. We can take the film down to the main library and you can do what you have to do.'

'But how will you travel without a car? Is it far?'

'The least you know, the better at this stage. You're working as an operative. We're using standard practice. Do you understand?'

She nodded.

'I'm going to take my bag now and leave you to make your way home by the usual route. You're to stay in the village until I come back in a few days. Go about your life in a normal way. Don't change your daily pattern. At some point, I will call you. You're to answer as you normally would unless you're being forced to do so. It's unlikely, but if you are being held, and used as a decoy for example, you will answer "Hello. Yes?" Not just "Hello." Got it?'

Lottie echoed, 'Hello. Yes?'

'Good. It's known as a duress code. To show I understand I'll also reply in the same way and I'll assume something has gone wrong and you're speaking under duress.'

Chapter Twenty-Nine

Cecil needed to get to London as soon as possible, but how? The railway stations at Chester, Shrewsbury and Euston were probably staked out and the local car hire firms would be alerted. There used to be a transport café three miles back on the A5, the other side of town. Yes that was it; the Tollgate Transport Café, with a long lay-by. *Hopefully it's still there. Could I use my warrant to persuade a London-bound truckie to give me a lift? Possibly, but a stranger cadging a lift, even with some official looking documents, won't ring true somehow. It's more likely a driver will refuse and call the local police at the first chance. But there are other ways of getting a lift on a truck. How to get to the transport café, that's the question. The A5 will be watched and there'll be police patrols and, anyway, it would take me back through Llangollen. I need to get off the road.*

Picking up his bag and taking a path he knew from the past, running parallel with the road, he set off overland, skirting the town. It would be difficult through thickly wooded and hilly terrain, but he should reach the Tollgate lay-by within a couple of hours or so.

He came down from the pine trees, ignoring the burn in his knee, making his way toward the road through the thick undergrowth of larch saplings and heather. There had been a light shower, soaking the undergrowth and saturating his shoes and trousers. A blue and yellow police car went by heading west with its prominent red "*HEDDLU*" sign. He crouched behind a rowan bush. *Perhaps they're on the lookout for me.* He studied the setting before him. A low drystone wall bounded the road. Yes, it was still there. The café building was constructed of large stone slabs similar to the wall but most interesting among the commercial vehicles parked up in the lay-by were between fifteen and twenty articulated lorries all with semi-trailers. They were mostly facing east and the route to the M54, M6 and London, with cars and small vans among them. The smell of cooking, frying onions and bacon fat, reminded him that first he needed to eat in preparation for a trying journey.

He pushed through the doors into an ante-room with a notice-board displaying a handwritten sign on a large sheet of paper commanding *"DO NOT USE THIS PLACE AS AN OFFICE"*. He entered the main room of the café. It was a space with a generous spread of faded brown Formica tables crowded with truckers, van drivers, car owners, and their passengers. Giving the place a cautious scan, he joined the queue at the self-service counter and chose from the menu board sausage, egg, bacon, chips, beans, and a large mug of black tea. Taking his piled plate, he sat at a small corner table where he could look out of the windows over the lay-by, watching truck arrivals and departures as he ate. In particular, he was looking for a box trailer with rigid sides and not one with canvas sides nor, indeed, a refrigerated trailer.

He had almost finished eating when he stiffened with shock. A police patrol car came towards the lay-by from the west about to pull in. A police officer got out of the passenger side and came into the café carrying a sheet of paper.

Chapter Thirty

Looking fixedly ahead at the reflection in the window, Cecil saw the officer enter the dining room. He glanced around before going over to the counter and speaking to a member of staff. To Cecil's intense relief, he left.

As the police car pulled away, he saw a truck with a box trailer arriving from the west. He waited until the driver had parked up and entered, then he slipped out of the room. In the ante-room he was confronted by his own image on a poster pinned on the noticeboard asking "*HAVE YOU SEEN THIS MAN?*" Not stopping to read the smaller details, he left and walked around the building to the wall. Checking the lay-by was clear, he moved along the space between the wall and the trucks, examining the trailer fastenings of those facing east with London signage. He selected one with lettering featuring Deptford. The long draw bars fastening the double doors were not sealed nor locked, so the trailer was not carrying a valuable load, perhaps just empty containers or pallets.

The clamp was easily lifted, then the bolt was unlatched and the draw bar dropped as quietly as possible. He edged the door open enough for him to take a look inside. He was right. There was adequate room among the secured stacks of pallets. Tossing in his bag and grunting with the pain of his protesting knee, he hauled himself up and drew the door to, plunging himself into semi-darkness. It was relieved by the pale light coming in from gaps in the trailer body. With the help of his mobile phone light he found a length of cord with one end tied to the slats along the trailer side. He used this to secure the doors by tying it to the other end. He hoped the driver wouldn't check them before he pulled away. If he did he'd be locked in the dark for the duration of the journey, maybe longer.

Chapter Thirty-One

Lottie arrived back at her house feeling shaken and unsettled. She would sit down with a cup of tea and think things over. The thought was still in her mind as she entered her living room.

'Hello, Miss Williams-Parry.' The man sitting in her easy chair uncrossed his legs. 'My name is Guy Hackett. I expect Cecil has told you about me.' He pointed to the other chair. 'Please sit down.'

She stood motionless, becoming aware of movement in other rooms and someone talking behind her. Now the house seemed full of people. Two men came in from the kitchen. One of them took her arm, leading her firmly to the chair. Taking her laptop, he passed it to someone at the door. The other took her rucksack from her and began to unpack it, delving with expert hands. Her legs felt weak, as if they couldn't hold her, and she collapsed onto the chair.

'As we were in the area, we thought we would give you a call, but it seems you were out, so we waited.' Hackett lit a cigarette and drew on it deeply before expelling the smoke at the ceiling in one short puff. 'Actually, it had occurred to us that you may be quite useful given what you know about the place, the village, and so on.' He contemplated his cigarette before turning his eyes on her with a keen stare. 'I'm going to ask you two things. Firstly, to go into your front room where one of my female colleagues will carry out a body search and, secondly, to come along with us where I feel sure you will wish to cooperate in answering certain questions. You need have no concerns about your house or your car. We'll need to take your laptop for a short while, though, but when we've finished here, your things will be left secure and in perfect order, just as we found them.'

On the road, at the bottom of the drive, a black-windowed car waited. Strong hands ushered her inside to sit between two anonymous men. Before it pulled away, Hackett spoke in the driver's ear, 'Go by a roundabout route, taking a couple of hours. You know the drill.'

Chapter Thirty-Two

At Oswestry

Hackett leaned back in his chair. 'Miss Lottie Williams-Parry,' he paused. 'I shall call you Lottie, if you don't mind.'

Lottie remained silent. She had been pushed into an old armchair with failed springs and a Rexene cover that chilled her. There was a smell of must in the room. Cold terror had taken hold, draining her of freedom, of action.

After a pause, Hackett went on soothingly, 'I must say, Lottie, I'm rather intrigued as to how Cecil persuaded you to join him. We know he stayed at your house for a short while at least. Oh, please don't deny it. Among other things, we found two bowls and two spoons on your draining board.' He paused for a moment. 'You must realise by now that he's unhinged.'

She tried to say something but she didn't know what.

Hackett took out his handkerchief, removed his spectacles and began meticulously polishing them. Lifting his head from his task he carefully hooked the wire frame around his ears and with one finger adjusted them on the bridge of his nose. Turning the full force of his gaze upon her, ignoring the spasm in his eye, he said, 'We need to know where you have just come from. Was it Llangollen, perhaps? And we also need to know what Cecil was doing in the town, where he was going and so on.'

Lottie remained silent, trying to make sense of the thoughts and feelings swirling around inside her.

'He went to pick up something, didn't he?'

Should she tell him?

'What was it?'

She opened her mouth but confusion robbed her of speech.

Hackett stared. His cold blue eyes seemed to create an almost unbearable tension in the room. The door behind her was opened and Hackett looked up. She heard someone say, 'Sir', urgently as if to call him over. He rose. 'I have to deal with other things right now. In the meantime, we're going to give you a room to yourself for a while – leave you to think things over. Later we'll have questions to put to you again. We need to be satisfied with your answers. Think carefully about that.' He stood up. 'Time is running out and we're getting rather anxious.'

Chapter Thirty-Three

As the truck moved off Cecil eased the door open, just enough to let in some light, and lashed it in position with the cord. Soon the border was crossed near Oswestry and the chain of roundabouts by-passing Shrewsbury was behind them as they joined the M54.

After about one and a half hours on the M6, the truck joined the M1 and began to slow as it approached what Cecil realised was a service station. Dusk was closing in but there was enough light for him to see the sign, "*Watford Gap*". Discretion prompted him to close the door before the truck pulled in and parked up. After an hour, the truck was on its way again, rolling south through the night. Cecil decided to leave the door closed and settle down on the floor using his bag as a pillow. He lay trying to come to terms with the thoughts and feelings ebbing and flowing through his mind. *Six full days since arriving at the cemetery. Six full days since I've been taken to the grave of the boy I discovered in the newspaper cutting, my predecessor bearing my own name, unpacking my past, releasing these thoughts, these feelings to rise from deep within. A past hidden from me. At the coffee bar, the attempt on my life and the unpleasant meeting with Hackett.*

Cecil became aware that this was where his idea to release the contents of the microfilms into the public arena hardened into a fierce and ruthless determination. The meeting with Voronov, his shooting. *That was meant for me.* The bog. On the run over the moors. Those SVR goons. Lottie coming on the scene and the business with the Russians – with her help. She came just at the right time.

His thoughts of Lottie prompted conflicting emotions. There was satisfaction at the way he had made use of her. Seizing the opportunity proved that he'd lost none of his ability for exploiting a situation as it presented itself. And yet, something nagged at him; something that pulled at him in a persistent way, difficult to express. There was her trust in him, even the beginnings of affection, perhaps. He felt safe and comfortable with that. Then there was the way she laid her past bare, how she'd been susceptible to abuse, to being used, deceived and betrayed. Was he not also guilty of using her? The question crept into his mind unbidden. Is that what he wanted to do? A short while ago the answer would have been yes but now . . .

He recalled his feelings when their hands touched and how she'd impelled him to reveal his own story about the discovery of his predecessor's death when the grave prompted his crisis of identity. Somehow that little boy's grave had linked them, in a way he couldn't explain. The thought left him feeling uneasy as he slipped into sleep.

He was awakened by the juddering of the trailer as it lurched from side to side dislodging fine choking dust. This was followed by a blast of compressed air and silence. It was broken when he heard the cab door slam and the driver moving around outside. Cecil assumed he was disconnecting cables and held his breath in case he came around to the rear and noticed the unbolted doors.

Instead, there was the sound of metal on metal as the landing gear legs were let down. The front end of the trailer tipped a little as it was winched off the articulated joint of the tractor mounting. Then the cab door of the tractor unit was opened and shut followed by the engine starting up. He heard it moving away, leaving his world to darkness and the muffled sounds of the night punctuated by the mournful note of a ship's horn. He hoped it was somewhere out on the Thames.

Chapter Thirty-Four

Lottie's eyes ranged restlessly around the windowless room. Long ago the walls had been painted green but now large scabs of flaking paint were hanging down, exposing the plaster. The once-white ceiling had faded to a dull yellow. There were rusty pipes running along where the wall met the low ceiling. The floor was covered in worn brown linoleum and the room was lit by a green glass pendant lamp infested with spider webs and dead flies. There were some rusty filing cabinets along one wall. It was the only furniture except the uncomfortable chair on which she was sitting, facing the institutional-looking door. She knew it was locked, even though she hadn't moved from the chair since she'd been conducted into the room. She'd heard the key turning as they left.

The air was cold and damp. She had no idea where she was. The journey had taken a long time. They'd taken her watch and phone but she didn't think she'd been there long. Closing her eyes to keep out the sights in the room, she tried to concentrate on the thoughts swirling around in her head. Going over the events of the last few hours seemed to steady her feelings as she tried to make sense of them.

Was Huw Cecil mentally deranged, as Hackett had said?

He seemed so normal, and yet so driven by something. Anyone could see that. Was it to accuse the people on the microfilm or was that only part of it? He's shown his feelings. Deeply troubled they are and it's clear he's desperate to assert himself in some way. Perhaps exposing the film lay behind his strange determination – his passion almost. And is this man Hackett going to put it to the right use? He's part of the security services, after all. A feeling of dread settled in the pit of her stomach. *Have I made a terrible mistake? Have I assisted in the murder of innocent people? Although the man Huw shot at the coffee bar* did *point a gun at him. And those men at the cemetery, they were treating him roughly – did they have to die by Huw bursting into violence in such a terrible way? Why didn't he call the proper people when he'd dealt with them? Oh God, I've only got his word, after all. But somehow it seems true. Surely he couldn't have made up the stories about the children, the young girls, could he . . .?*

The sound of a key turning crashed into her thoughts. The door was opened and one of the two men from before gestured to her. 'Please come with me.'

She got up stiffly and followed him along the passage until he opened the door of the previous room. At the end of the passage she knew was the outside door, and freedom. She had a sudden urge to shove past him and make a run for it but it passed with a feeling of hopelessness as she realised the door was probably locked.

Hackett was sitting in the same chair. He pointed to the other one. 'Please sit down.' Anxiety seemed to have sharpened her perception. Her watch, rucksack, official wallet, and her phone were on the table between them. A small open-topped polystyrene box lay at the side of her phone, arousing her curiosity. There was a plate of sandwiches, a chrome teapot, and a small jug of milk. Also two cups and a bowl of sugar lumps with tiny tongs.

Despite this, she was not calmed and the room still smelt of must.

Hackett gestured to the table. 'You may take your things but we need to keep your phone near me.' He pointed to it. 'We've enhanced its send and receive facility so that you can speak on it from a distance while we can listen in. Should it ring, you will not answer until I or my colleagues tell you what to say. This little box,' he held it up, 'is a muffle. When we place it over the phone we can speak to you without being picked up by the phone.'

There was a moment of silence between them in which Lottie's mind lapsed into numbness before Hackett spoke again. 'Is there anything you would like to ask?'

'Where am I and why am I here?'

'You are here to help us, Lottie. It may take a little time – perhaps more than a little. We've made arrangements for you to stay the night with us. Don't worry, I'm sure you'll be quite comfortable in your own room but you *will* have someone with you at all times in case your phone goes off. In the morning, we'll need some answers to some questions. When we are satisfied, you will be taken home and we can show our appreciation of your work for us. Do have some tea before you go to your room. You will find reading material there. I hope it's to your satisfaction. Dinner is at eight. You will be called.'

Chapter Thirty-Five

Cecil must have dozed off, because he was becoming aware of faint morning light through the gaps in the bodywork. Easing open the trailer door, he peered out. There was no one in sight. He was in a depot of some sort with many other box trailers lined up in ranks.

Getting down he made his way, still with his bag, along the wall, trailer by trailer, until he could see the entrance gates. They were open but there was a security cabin. Approaching it from the blind side, Cecil bent double as he passed below the window and out of the gates into a wide and busy street. It was alive with early morning bustle and clamour. Looking one way, the distant view was closed by the gigantic purple sign for a *Premier Inn*. In the other direction it was marred by an ugly concrete bridge straddling the wide road. Using his phone map, he read his location as Deptford and the concrete structure he could see was Deptford Bridge, a station on the Docklands Light Railway, elevated above the street.

Hackett would be unaware he had reached London yet, he thought, though he would suspect that's where he was going when he disappeared from the scene. So he may have contacted Thames House as a precaution. For the time being Cecil felt he was below the radar. Apart from the mainline stations, there was nowhere else they would expect him to be – they knew he wouldn't be at his house. Now he had to plot his route to the Tooting Broadway address.

Taking the Docklands Light Railway, he got out at Canary Wharf, aiming to change to the Jubilee Line. It was as he was crossing the crowded open space of the vast interior of the new station that he felt the feelings of vulnerability descending on him, like a cold damp sheet.

On the platform, he used the reflection in the glass screen doors to make a close examination of the press of people for a carriage length along the platform. As the train drew in and the doors opened, he stepped to one side, letting the crowd go, making sure there was no one left. He took the next one to London Bridge, waiting until the doors started to close before getting up quickly. He stepped off, changing to a Northern Line train going towards Morden before finally leaving it at Tooting Broadway.

Buying a roll and a drink from a fast food stall as he was leaving the station on Tooting High Street, he joined the departing throng. Stepping to one side at the front of the statue of Edward the Seventh before the glazed modernist façade of the station, he kept its massive pedestal to his back. While he ate and drank, he scrutinised the people hurrying by on either side. If anyone was following, they would be caught unawares. Then he used his phone map to locate Broad Road.

Chapter Thirty-Six

It took only a few minutes to walk along the wide busy high street, flanked by newly built apartment blocks and offices, to come to the junction with Broad Road. Modern glazed white buildings towered on either side, as if forming an entrance. These gave way to a high brick walls and tall Edwardian school buildings running to a distant junction at the end of the street. The other side was lined with parked cars and semi-detached houses built in the nineteen-twenties. Now they were plastic double-glazed with refuse bins in their front gardens and low walls in an incongruous variety of masonry, depending on which decade the houses were 'improved'.

He soon found number eighty-one. It still had its original nineteen-twenties front door with an opaque pane of coloured glass in the upper panel. Layers of peeling paint exposed patches of bare wood. Glancing up and down the street, he was conscious of his heartbeat increasing as he started along the path.

There was a tall gate at the side of the house. He tried the latch but it was bolted. Putting down his bag for a moment, he stepped onto the low adjoining wall, wincing at the brief sting of pain and peered over the gate. The passage was clear. He approached the front door with a strong feeling of unease. What was he going to find behind it? This was the end of the trail, he hoped, as he pressed the bell. It rang. There was no response. He pressed it again. Somewhere in the house there was vague movement. He listened to the footsteps shuffling along the passage until he could see a moving shape distorted by the cloudiness of the glass panel. The door shuddered ajar just enough for a hand with parchment-like skin to clasp the frame and let the wrinkled face of a woman some years past middle age peer around through strands of grey hair. She removed a cigarette that seemed reluctant to leave the blue lower lip of her slack mouth. Cecil suffered the scrutiny of her rheumy eyes for some seconds. 'Mrs Wilkinson?'

'Yes?'

'You have a package for Mr Smith?'

'Have you got the fifty pounds?' she asked with an alacrity that belied her appearance.

Cecil took the notes out of his pocket and held each one up for her to see.

Without a word, the face disappeared and the door was closed. Cecil stood in apprehension, wondering what to expect when she returned, or even if it was ever to be opened to him again.

Feeling vulnerable, he stole a look around the side of the house. Soon, the shuffling footsteps returned and the door was opened just a little more than before. She stood with a small cardboard carton in one hand and held out the other. 'Let's see the money again.'

'Open it first,' commanded Cecil.

Giving him a malevolent look, she clawed with stiff fingers at the tape that sealed the carton. She pulled the lid open and held it up to him. Inside was a metal container the size of a box of kitchen matches. He seized it before she could close the lid with her claw-like hands.

'The money!' she screamed.

He unlatched the lid, releasing a waterproof seal. Inside were ten minute cylindrical canisters in two ranks of five. He picked out one canister, pulled off the sealing tape, and drew out a short length of black film. It seemed genuine, though there was no way he could be sure. He replaced the canister, shut the container and put it back in the carton. Thrusting the money into an outstretched talon, he turned on his heel and walked down the path, all the time conscious of sharp eyes boring into his back.

He had it. He had the microfilm. Triumph welled up but it was quickly replaced by exhaustion, leaving him drained and physically limp. He was in no shape to get back to Lottie. Needing to rest up, he would take a room down the road in the *Premier Inn*. It should be safe enough. There was no way he could be traced in London. In the morning, he would buy a cheap phone, hire a car using his own documents, and set off early.

Chapter Thirty-Seven

After a restless and exhausting night, tossing about on a cold damp bed, Lottie lay awake, looking at the faint dawn light coming through inadequate curtains. She became aware of sounds she realised had been there all along. There were doors opening and closing, footsteps advancing and retreating, and a faint droning. It reminded her of machinery, or some kind of radio equipment. There was a woman sitting at a table in the corner. Lottie tried to ignore her but it wasn't possible. It was the same woman who had searched her and had taken the first watch. Lottie assumed someone else had been taking turns with her through the night.

As the room became lighter, she turned in the bed to stare at her minder, examining her features closely for the first time. She was tall, with close-cropped hair set in a straight fringe across a narrow forehead above sharp features. The low chair on which she was sitting emphasised her angular build and heavy shoes made her feet seem too large for her thin legs. Lottie took some satisfaction in her unease at being stared at.

There was a single knock on the door. The minder got to her feet. 'Come on. Time to get up.' She waited outside while Lottie went into the tiny washroom and dressed. Without a word, she was led along a harshly lit windowless passage. Her footsteps echoed on the cold terrazzo floor. They came to a door leading into a room with a long table set with a large plate of toast, two bowls of cereal, a milk jug, and a pot of tea. Taking a chair, Lottie's minder joined her at the table, placing the phone and muffle between them. They

131

breakfasted in silence. Lottie didn't feel like eating but she thought it best to try in order to keep up her strength and perhaps to clear the dull headache she'd had since she arrived.

As she munched her toast, it was clear that her minder was enjoying breakfast no more than she was. Pushing her plate away, she glanced at her watch and turned to Lottie. 'When you've finished, I'd like you to come with me.'

'Where are we going?' She was swept by a sudden wave of apprehension.

'Mr Hackett wants to talk to you. It won't take long. Then you'll be taken home.'

Not feeling at all reassured, Lottie followed her minder back along the passage past the washroom until she was led to an open door.

A genial voice called, 'Ah, Lottie!' Hackett was sitting behind a table on the opposite side of a small bare room. 'Do come in and sit down.' He was flanked on either side by two of the men she'd seen at her house.

As she entered, her minder went over to the table and placed the phone and muffle on it. As she left the room, the door closed followed by the loud click of a lock.

Hackett was pointing to an uncomfortable-looking chair facing him and set some distance from the table. Lottie approached it apprehensively. Her knees felt weak as she sat down.

He remained still with his hands resting on the table, palms down, his face expressionless. For some uncomfortable seconds Lottie was subjected to his disconcerting stare until finally he spoke. His voice was incisive, almost hushed, 'This is an interview and nothing said in this room is being recorded. Mr Lessing and Mr Kerr here are assisting me.' He took out a packet of cigarettes. 'Would you like one,' he offered.

Lottie shook her head.

Hackett took his time lighting up and drew hard before expelling the smoke at the ceiling. 'Are you warm enough? This old building can be chilly. I'm told it's due for demolition.'

She could only manage a slight nod.

'I hope you slept as well as possible under the circumstances. And the breakfast?' He raised his eyes and tried to force a chuckle but it came out as a snigger, 'Surely it couldn't have been worse than mine.'

After a pause, Hackett glanced at a file on the table before him. It was the only object on it, apart from a carafe of water and two glasses. He looked up. 'You do know why you are here?'

Lottie was about to blurt out 'no' before she realised she had a good idea what this was all about. During her restless night she had gone into her circumstances over and over, especially the question of whether Huw had told the truth about the microfilm, or whether this Hackett man was telling the truth. She decided silence was best, for now at least.

Hackett waited some moments for an answer before going on, 'We do appreciate what you've done for us up to now and we hope you can help us some more.' He paused. 'So I'm going to put some questions to you and when you have provided us with satisfactory answers it will be time for you to be taken home.'

I'll give him the kind of answers he wants. Anything to get this over with.

He opened the file. 'Let's see what we *do* know . . .' He ran his finger down the first page before looking up. 'Miss Lottie Williams-Parry, you were recruited as a contact and, as such, you reported the email Cecil sent you requesting the location of a grave. The report came to me, actually. You showed considerable initiative following him to the coffee bar and reporting the incident. I think my colleagues will agree.' He looked to each one who nodded in turn. 'And now we come to the information that is both mystifying and intriguing. Certainly it is so to my colleagues and I, if not to you, for it seems you met him a second time.'

Stubbing out his cigarette he placed his hands on the table and leaned forward.

Again Lottie became conscious of his eyes glaring through the lenses of his spectacles, like blue polished orbs.

'Perhaps you can help me. We know that Cecil met you for the

133

second time somewhere. We don't know where. But he made his way to your house and spent some time there.' Hackett sat back in his chair. 'So, I would like to know more about this.'

What should I tell him and where should I start?

He leaned forward again. 'There's something else I find intriguing. You see, you had your rucksack packed for a day or two with your phone charger, yet you arrived at your house without anything being disturbed. I doubt whether it had been opened. You'd been somewhere. Now, I ask myself, why would anyone drive off with a bag packed for a few days and return within an hour or so?' He leaned back. His bald head gleamed in the pale light. 'I wonder where you thought you were going?'

Still she remained silent. After all he hadn't asked her any direct questions yet.

Abruptly his tone became sharp and his voice became rasping. 'Where *were* you going, Lottie?'

Taken by surprise, she stiffened.

He went on, 'We've been talking to Mr Edwards, your neighbour from the house next door. He saw a man of Cecil's description getting in your car, with you driving.'

Hackett took out another cigarette and went through the process of lighting it before cradling his elbow in his hand as he released smoke to one side, never taking his eyes off Lottie. 'You've been used. You may not realise it yet, but you have. Cecil has used you, your house, and your car. Oh, you may see it as helping him. Perhaps you think you're both in it together, thwarting the evil designs of the dark forces. But let me remind you: you have taken up with the Security Service, agreeing to work with us as a part-time employee. *And* you have signed Section One of the Official Secrets Act. Unless you help us, you will find yourself in trouble of the most serious kind.'

Lottie felt sick. This was not how she had seen it. It had all happened so quickly, with little time to think. *Huw was so convincing, so why am I hesitating? Why am I holding back from telling all? Is it because he also convinced me of the likely danger from Hackett?*

134

Hackett's voice broke into her thoughts. 'Shall we try again?'

Lottie remained silent, focusing her gaze on the patterns of the dusty frosted glass in the window panes above his head.

'Very well. This is what I think happened. Somehow, Cecil persuaded you to drive him into Llangollen in your car. You don't need to go into the details of how he managed to do so, just confirm that is what happened.'

Still silence from Lottie.

'A nod will suffice.'

She used all her strength locking the muscles in her neck and biting the inside of her cheek to resist the urge to respond to his persuasive tone.

But Hackett's voice wouldn't allow that. He ignored her silence. 'For some reason you left him there and went home.'

Lottie stared up at the ceiling above his head trying to shut him out by concentrating on the shapes in the damp patches.

There was a stillness between them lasting some moments until it was broken by the scrape of the ashtray as Hackett leaned over to scribble out his half-smoked cigarette. The sound jarred on Lottie's nerves. He glanced sideways at Lessing and sat back. 'I suppose Cecil has given you the story about information of a compromising kind.' He paused before going on, 'He's a sick man under the delusion that we wish to suppress it.'

Was it so? It seemed to Lottie her thoughts acquired a voice as she blurted out, 'If it's just a story, why don't you go to the police?'

Hackett remained calm. 'Do you know he caused the deaths of three men on the moor two days ago?'

So it was true what happened on the moor. Just as Huw said, but he would have been killed if they'd caught him.

'You saw for yourself what he's capable of at the village coffee bar. I don't need to convince you he's a dangerous man but what you don't know is he's unhinged, disturbed, suffering from delusions, on the point of going downright mad.'

Was it true what he said? Was Huw disturbed in some way? If so, was she also on the edge of madness, for she had taken part in the dreadful business – she

135

couldn't bring herself to even think the word "killing" – *at the cemetery lane? Something they knew nothing about. Should I tell them about it? No, I won't.* Somehow, holding on to the information gave her the feeling she still had some control.

Hackett went on, 'Now he's loose and dangerous to the general public and you've assisted him.' He leaned forward, tapping the table to emphasise his words. 'If we bring in the police, you could be charged right now with being an accessory to murder.' He leaned back again. 'But we won't do that because you're still on our books and you've been invaluable in this difficult situation, acting as you did, as a double asset.' He turned to the other two. 'Is that not right, gentlemen?' They both nodded.

Lottie was confused. 'What do you mean?'

'I'm throwing you a lifeline, Lottie. Come back on board.' He paused to let the words sink in. 'This is how I see it – oh, feel free to correct me if I'm wrong – you took Cecil to your house and agreed to drive him into Llangollen. There he gave our watchers the slip and picked up a package from somewhere. Then he left you and you went back to your house. Now to complete the operation all you have to do is tell us where he has gone with the package.'

What should I say? I've no idea where he's gone, he's made sure of that. 'I don't know,' she whispered in a failing voice.

'What was that?' He turned his head as if straining to listen. 'You don't know?'

'He didn't tell me,' she almost shouted.

Hackett stood up and came around the table. He leaned over and placed his face close to hers. 'You know,' he breathed softly so there was a strong smell of tobacco, 'I'm all that stands between you and a charge of being an accessory to multiple murders. It is in your interests to work with us.'

Lottie stared back at him with a look that revealed the terror sweeping over her. 'I don't know,' she stammered. 'I just don't know.'

He stood up and went back to sit in his chair. His voice cold, he asked, 'Did he tell you what the package contained?'

Lottie hesitated. 'Yes.'

'Well, that's why we're after it. We want the people on the micro-film to be held to account. As you know, he thinks we're going to destroy it. It turns out he suffered a catastrophic experience in the late nineties. It was before my time as his case officer.' He shook his head. 'He'd just reached forty. Tragic for a promising career snuffed out so early. Personally, I thought he was unsuitable for this task.' He shrugged. 'But the decision was out of my hands. It's probably what's behind his extraordinary behaviour. He's paranoid, Lottie. He feels he's a victim and that people are plotting against him. It's possible he's been sliding towards a breakdown for some time. Something has sent him over the edge.'

At this point, Hackett took out another cigarette and lit it, drawing deeply as Lottie had seen him do before. 'As a matter of interest, where *did* he pick up the package? Somewhere in the town?' He plucked a flake of tobacco from his tongue. 'You might as well tell me.'

Lottie decided not to answer. She wouldn't have been able to explain why. Something in Hackett's manner. Perhaps his disdainful arrogance?

He shrugged. 'No matter. It has no bearing one way or another.' He drew on his cigarette, thoughtfully puffing out smoke. 'So, you were driving and he was at the side of you with the package. What size would you say it was?'

Lottie hesitated.

Hackett placed his cigarette in the ashtray. 'Was it small like this?' He showed with his hands. 'Or much larger?' He opened them wider.

What can I say? I've no idea what size it's supposed to be. 'It wasn't a package,' she heard herself announcing.

Hackett froze.

'It was an envelope.'

'An envelope!' His voice was ice-cold. 'What was in it?'

'I think it was empty.'

'So, he opened it and . . .'

'There was something written on the inside. I don't know what.'

'An address?'

'I don't know. He wouldn't tell me.'

'Let's say it was an address. What did he do after he read it?'

Lottie wavered. *What shall I tell him? What have I told him so far?* She tried to think but Hackett was one step ahead of her. 'You're not being straight with me, Lottie. Instead of trying to remember what you've told me so far, just answer my question. What did he do after he read it?'

She couldn't remember. *Was it before we stopped, or after?*

'I'm trying to make it easy for you, Lottie.'

Lottie shook her head. 'I can't remember.'

'Well now, let's assume you left the town on the A5 – driving which way? Towards London, is that it?' He slammed his hand down on the table and in a loud rasping voice repeated, 'Is that it?'

She became aware of how uncomfortable the chair was. Her back was aching, there was a sharp pain in her side and she had a terrible thirst. She felt out of control, beside herself. 'Yes,' she cried. Her voice was almost hysterical.

'Thank you.' Now calm, the rhythm of the questioning broken, Hackett turned to Kerr. 'Alert the Office he's been on his way since yesterday afternoon.'

Kerr rose and went to the door behind her. After a light knock, it opened for him and he left the room.

'Now, Lottie, at some point you dropped him off and went back home. Correct?'

With her eyes cast down she nodded.

'Is there any reason why he would want to contact you again or have you seen the last of him?'

She didn't answer.

'Come on, Lottie.'

Shall I tell him? Wouldn't it be best just to believe what he said about Huw? Perhaps Huw is in some way suffering from a sort of mental condition . . .

Hackett took up his cigarette and, with one last draw, he stubbed it out while he released the smoke toward her. 'I'm disappointed in you, Lottie. I hoped you would be eager to help us. You could be home quickly.' He shrugged. 'Instead it looks as if we have to treat you as hostile – keep you here as long as it takes.' Leaning toward her he said, 'I may even have to put you into the hands of my more physical colleagues. One way or another, you *will* assist completely. You have one last chance: help the authorities and gain the appropriate thanks or shield a madman and face the consequences as an accomplice.'

Lottie's eyes grew wide and her breathing quickened with shock, but somehow she felt detached. *Something isn't right. I've done nothing wrong, nothing deserving this sort of thing.* A small seed of anger began to bloom in her chest. She was not going to let herself be used again. This time she would decide to take control.

Suddenly the phone rang, making everyone flinch. All eyes turned to it and, for a moment, movement in the room was stilled.

Chapter Thirty-Eight

Hackett snapped at her, 'Answer it.'

She was calm now and knew what she would say. It came out in a steady voice. 'Hello. Yes?'

Cecil paused for what seemed an eternity. 'Hello. Yes?' His voice uncertain, he asked, 'Where are you?'

She knew he was alerted. There was no going back now.

Hackett clapped the muffle over the phone. 'Tell him you're at your house and ask him has he got the film.'

What shall I say, Lottie thought. *I'll be as vague as possible and play the part.* 'I'm here at my place. Have you got it?'

Cecil's voice seemed to fill the room. 'On my way to you. I should be there in a couple of hours.'

Frustrated, Hackett muffled the phone again demanding, 'The film – ask him again.'

'Have you got the film?'

'I'll be a couple of hours. Be there,' came the reply. The call ended.

Hackett turned to Lessing who had his phone pressed to his ear. 'Location?' he demanded curtly.

'GCHQ give his position on the A5 just off the M54.'

At that moment Kerr came in and announced, 'Thames House alerted.'

Hackett acknowledged the information. Nodding towards the door, he led Kerr out of the room, closing it behind him. Keeping his voice down, he said, 'Cecil's on his way back from London. He should be at her house in a couple of hours, so he's travelling by car. We must assume he's got the film, though I don't know what he's got planned for it, or why he's coming back to her place. He must have some further use for the woman, so get over there with Lessing – just the two of you, so as not to overcrowd the place. And park your car well away out of sight, even if it means a long walk. He's supposed to be unsuspecting, but I won't take a chance. I'll have the security personnel standing by over here. The Duty Officer will be in charge.'

'What about the woman?'

'I'll follow shortly with her. I'd rather keep her close. We'll put her in the bathroom. It's at the rear of the house, upstairs. Take one of the tech boys to follow you with his own transport. Get him to secure the window. Make sure the door can't be locked from the inside and fit bolts on the outside. That should keep her out of the way. After that send him back here. Oh, and put a chair in there. We won't skimp on comfort.'

'What about after . . . you know. What do we do with her then?'

'I'll see that you'll both know what to do when the time comes. Oh, and do make sure Lessing brings some lengths of cord with him. You know the type.'

Hackett went back into the room. Sitting in his chair he faced Lottie with his eyes unfocused. *Why didn't Cecil stay in London? He has the film. Why is he coming back here to her house?* Hackett was afraid. He was afraid of failure but most of all he was afraid of Cecil.

She found the vacant stare of his cold eyes unnerving. It was making her tremble. *What am I going to do?* Anger had been quickly replaced by anxiety. She shut her eyes in an attempt to distance herself from the situation. As if from afar she heard the clink of glass, and water being poured. Sensing Hackett advancing on her, she heard him ask, 'What part are you playing in his plans, Lottie?'

Lottie opened her eyes, though she continued to tremble.

'You seem nervous. Please relax. Here, take this.' She ignored it, so he set the glass down in front of her. 'As I promised: you're going home. You'll be with me, of course, so I can keep an eye on you during the closing stages of this operation. We'll soon have Cecil and the film in the bag and we'll be of no further trouble to you.' He looked at her, sitting head bowed, and paused for a moment before continuing slowly and precisely, 'So you might as well tell me why he's coming back. As a pawn, what part are you playing in this endgame?' He placed his hands on the table, leaning towards her. 'Yes that's it. I should have realised: pawns can become important in the endgame. Come on, Lottie, tell me.'

Still she refused to respond.

Letting his breath out in a snort of exasperation, he stood up and went to the door.

Chapter Thirty-Nine

Cecil got out of the air-conditioned car into the dense sultry air of the afternoon. The weather had changed. The wind had gone, taking with it its nagging chill, leaving an oppressive stillness instead. Breathing deeply with his head down, he took a few minutes to let his jarred nerves settle before thinking what to do. It had been time to make the call, so, just after leaving the M54 westbound, he pulled into the lay-by on the A5. He hadn't expected Lottie to be taken. The duress code was just a precaution against a faint possibility. She'd implied she was speaking from her house, but was it true? They would have been listening, telling her what to say, and forcing her in some way. *They'll expect me to come after her.* He felt a surge of guilt and anxiety. *Christ! It's because of me she's held hostage in her own house.*

He looked up, shading his eyes from the white disc of the sun shining against a leaden sky. There, across the Shropshire Plain, the distant Wrekin rose through the heat haze, calming and steadying. *I have one advantage. Hackett and his team don't know I've been alerted. They think I'm walking into a baited trap. Then why go for her? Why not leave them to it? It would take some time for them to work out I wasn't coming. After all, I've got the film. Wouldn't it be better to abandon the library idea, to go back to London and find some other way of getting it out on social media? It would mean leaving her, leaving Lottie, but when they realised the trap was sprung, she'd be no good to them – they'd just let her go – wouldn't they? Like hell they would. She knew too much. They'd dispose of her. Yes, I'm certain of that. Anyway how the hell am I going to get the stuff online before they catch up with me, wherever I go? When I think about it, all avenues are blocked except her . . .*

As he looked at it from his present standpoint, he could see there was never going to be any other way of achieving what he set out to do. He was going to have to get her away from them for whatever reason, perhaps not just because it was expedient. Suddenly, as if taken off guard, the idea of her in the hands of those people tore him up.

Putting the thought to the back of his mind he got in the car to figure things out. He would take a small back lane that he knew from the past. It ran parallel with the main road on the other side of the derelict colliery. Then he would approach Lottie's house on foot, observing the situation from the cover of the spoil banks. It was two o'clock, with about two hours driving ahead of him. There was plenty of daylight left.

Chapter Forty

Lottie was walked up her drive with Lessing and Kerr on either side. As they passed her car, standing where she had left it, she heard Hackett driving off. She assumed it was to park his car out of sight.

When Hackett arrived at the door he met Lessing, who assured him Lottie was already secured. 'Tell Kerr to come into the front room,' he ordered.

When they gathered in the front room, Hackett settled himself on the piano stool and explained, 'I want one of you upstairs keeping watch from the front and, just in case, from the back. I'll be down here. If things are as expected, he should approach by car, coming up the road from the border. He'll park and come to the front door. When that happens, I want you, Kerr, taking cover at the side of the house so you can come round behind him when the door opens. We need to get him inside without a fuss. And you,' he addressed Lessing, 'I want you covering him from the top of the stairs as he's brought in. Is that clear?'

Hackett's phone chimed. Instinctively he sprang up from the piano stool and snatched it out, holding it close for some seconds before he held it for them all to hear. It was the Duty Officer at Oswestry. Thames House had just analysed a series of decrypted intercepts from GCHQ. They revealed that radio traffic between Yasenevo, Moscow, and the Russian Embassy in London showed the SVR were nonplussed by the loss of contact with their operatives on the ground in North Wales. They assumed they'd been taken out. Their last signal was the sighting of Cecil in the village.

Two further operatives had been despatched to pick up the trail. Radio silence was to be imposed until a further signal was received from London.

Hackett addressed them, 'You all heard that.' He sat down on the stool again thoughtfully lowering his chin to his chest. 'So that's where Cecil went after the business in the bog,' he mused. 'Over the moors to the village.' He lifted his head. 'But why?' He shrugged. 'Perhaps he was working his way around to Llangollen or perhaps to hide up for a while. Either way he must have had a hand in the disappearance of the Russians.' There was a hint of admiration in his voice.

After some moments of silence, which left the other two standing uneasily, Hackett seemed to shake himself. 'They should be well on their way here by now. The only clue they have is this house. After the shooting at the coffee bar, one of the others followed the woman here and reported it, so this will be their starting point.' He looked into their faces as if seeking inspiration. 'They may be watching it even now and monitoring our messages.' He took out his phone and, holding it out to them, he switched it off, gesturing for them to do the same. They followed suit.

He motioned for them to come closer. 'Success is almost within our grasp. I want to speak now, in our close group, about what I think is the best way to ensure it.' He paused, as if to let his words sink in. 'From now on, we will move forward without being monitored by our colleagues at Oswestry, and without having to refer back to Control at Thames House. No one will question how we achieved success when the film is in their hands. We are, after all, a deniable unit. Understood?'

Having spoken, Hackett looked them keenly in the face and, seeing no reason to elaborate, returned to the matter at hand, feeling free to express himself more directly as there was no monitoring. 'Now, I hope we take him alive because there's just a chance he doesn't have the film on him. He may have hidden it somewhere. In that case, we can try using the woman as a persuader but I don't think he's coming to rescue her out of the goodness of his heart. He

146

needs her for some reason and I haven't been able to get it out of her, not yet anyway. So we may have to use persuasion on him as well. Meanwhile I'll go up and have a word with her. It may be I can get her to cooperate and meet him at the door as he expects. That's why I've brought her. It would make our job much easier and safer.'

'If I might ask, sir?' Kerr spoke up. 'Would we be using the standard method of persuasion?'

'If necessary, yes.'

'Without authority, sir?'

'Yes. As I have just explained, we won't be referring back. We're keeping radio silence.' He dismissed the thought that authority would probably be withheld. 'These methods leave no marks, as you know, and I'll take full responsibility.' With that, Hackett stood up. 'Now get to it. You, Lessing, keep watch in the front bedroom. He should be here anytime. By the end of the day, we'll have this business in the bag.'

Lottie sat on the chair resting the back of her head against the wall. Swept by waves of anxiety, she kept her eyes closed, as if to shut out what was happening. Once they entered her house, all pretence of treating her as anything other than a prisoner had evaporated. She had been roughly conducted to her bathroom cell. She could still hear the bolts shooting home.

There were muffled voices. The bolts were moving again. Then Hackett entered. 'Oh, don't bother to get up.' Leaving the door open, he sat on the edge of the bath. 'Well, we can expect him to arrive at any minute now,' Fixing her with his eyes he went on, 'but before he does I'll ask you once more: will you tell me why he's coming back here?'

Lottie shook her head. 'I don't know.'

He opened his jacket to reveal his underarm holster with the ugly butt of the automatic pistol protruding. Partly drawing the weapon so that Lottie could see the dull metallic blue of the frame, he slipped it back. 'As you see, Lottie, we're prepared for anything Cecil can throw at us. You've seen him in action – you know what he's capable

147

of. We'll take no chances. If, on the other hand, he gives himself up quietly, he'll come to no harm. There'll be questions for him to answer, of course, but he could come out of it with little effect. The whole matter will be treated as what it is – a nervous breakdown. It's not surprising, given what he's been through.'

He leaned forward, making her feel uncomfortable, so that she turned her face from him, casting her eyes to the floor. Speaking in gentle hushed tones he said, 'Now, you can play a part in this, helping to bring things to a conclusion with everyone unhurt. It will also help to restore your position in the Service. If, when he comes to the door, he's met by you, it will make it easier to disarm him without a fight. We'll be close by and it'll all be over quickly before he can react. But without your help there'll be a nasty exchange of fire, and at three to one within this closed space there can be little doubt of the outcome. What do you say? There's no time to waste. He'll be here at any moment.'

What can I say thought Lottie. *It's obvious they think Huw's walking into a trap. He'll probably be expecting at least one of them at the door, if he comes to the door, and as Hackett said there'll be a nasty exchange of fire but not quite as he thinks because Huw will be ready and the readiness is all. Oh God! I hope that's so. I might as well go along with them. I don't want him to get hurt.* She looked up and nodded.

'Good.' Hackett stood up and went out to Lessing at the top of the stairs. 'Keep her in there until we're ready.'

Chapter Forty-One

Careful to avoid kicking up the loose black dust on the desolate landscape of the abandoned pit-bank, Cecil shaded his eyes from the punitive white glare of the late-afternoon sun. It was beating down, driving away colour, leaving only light and shadow. He'd left the car in the lane on the other side of the old colliery. Taking cover in a clump of bushes, he used a broken branch to scoop out a shallow hole in the cindery soil. Then he placed the carton holding the waterproof film stock container in it. As an afterthought, he put one of the phones in the carton before burying it and marking the spot with a slab of red shale. He was about to use Voronov's field glasses to scan the house but then he realised the sun might glint off them and announce his position, so he put them away. Nevertheless, he could detect no movement within. The house seemed empty, with Lottie's car on the drive facing it and no other vehicles in sight, just occasional traffic on the road. He settled back to watch and wait.

The bushes provided some shade, but at the cost of insects filling the air and seeking out his sweat as the shimmering heat rose from the sulphurous pit bank. He didn't have to wait long. Just as the temperature was becoming insufferable, he tensed as a car pulled up. Both Lessing and Kerr came out of the front door down the drive towards the car. Lottie got out and they escorted her back into the house, closing the door. The car moved off. Cecil waited some minutes and, as he expected, Hackett walked down the road and up the drive into the house.

So that's it: the trap's set. The high wall at the back of the house offers no prospect of an approach from the rear so it'll have to be a frontal attack. They expect me to arrive in a car coming from the east and I'll be under observation as soon as I draw up. If I come by any other way and from any other direction they'll be suspicious and I'll lose the initiative. That's what they expect, so that's what I'll have to do. As far as can be made out, there are three of them in the house as well as Lottie, Hackett, Lessing, and Kerr. Only Lottie knows I'm warned and she's expecting me to make my move. I can't let her down now. He felt a rising concern for her as his pulse began to race. *And I stand a good chance of getting to the front door before they find out but I'll have to walk straight up to it as if unsuspecting, without checking on the outside of the house, even though it goes against the grain. I'll have two, maybe three seconds. Hopefully that should be enough and with luck I should be able to seize the first one to appear and use him as a shield and a hostage, so avoiding a shooting match but, just in case . . .*

He checked his pistols one by one, slipped the safety, and left them loose in their holsters. Then he went for the car.

Chapter Forty-Two

'He's here!' Lessing called from the front bedroom. 'Just pulled up.'

'At last. I was beginning to wonder what was keeping him,' Hackett answered. 'Bring her down. And, Kerr, get round the side.'

Kerr nodded.

Lessing hurried Lottie down the stairs, holding her firmly by the shoulders. Hackett took her from him and stood her at the door. 'When he knocks, open it for him to come in,' he hissed in her ear. He moved back into the front room out of sight while Lessing, at the top of the stairs, brought up his gun and covered the door.

Lottie stood at the door, her muscles taut as she heard footsteps approaching. Should she call out a warning? She opened her lips but her tongue was sticking to the roof of her mouth. There was a pause and some shuffling. The tension was shattered as the doorknocker was lifted and brought down three times.

Hesitantly, with her heart thumping, Lottie unfastened the door and drew it open. It was Kerr's face she saw first, looking over Cecil's shoulder from behind with one hand resting on it. His other hand held a pistol with the muzzle poking in Cecil's ear.

Chapter Forty-Three

'Ah, Cecil! Do come in, we've been waiting for you.' Hackett moved forward and swiftly slipped handcuffs on his wrists before running his hands deftly over Cecil's jacket drawing out the Glock.

Continuing with the body search, he took out Voronov's field glasses, placing them on the hall table before resuming his search and quickly finding the Makarov. Handling the two guns gingerly, he slipped on the safety catches and passed them to Lessing who was coming down the stairs with his pistol pointing at Cecil. Hackett returned to his searching, bringing out mobile phone, car keys, warrant and cards.

Going over his flinching body with his fingertips, he addressed the others, 'He hasn't got it on him. Take the lady back to her room, Lessing, then get his car number checked and go over it in your usual way. Mr Cecil and I are going to have a little talk. This way, old boy.' Hackett indicated the door into the dining room. 'Kerr will set out the chairs at the table for us.' For a fleeting moment, Lottie's eyes locked with Cecil's conveying a look of helplessness and despair as she was hustled up the stairs.

Chapter Forty-Four

Cecil was placed at the dining table with his back to the fireplace. Hackett sat opposite with his back to the doors. The sun was lowering in the west. The day was drawing in.

'Do switch the light on, Kerr, and take your place. Oh, I feel I have to warn you, Cecil, Kerr will be sitting in the corner behind you on your right, his gun at the ready.' The bulb cast a cone of brightness out of its dusty white shade bathing the table and those around it in a pallid luminosity and casting lengthening shadows on the walls.

Cecil looked into Hackett's face opposite him, made ashen by the paleness of the electric light that turned his glasses into circular mirrors. The numbness at the shock of being captured was wearing off, though he could still feel the cold muzzle of Kerr's pistol in his ear. He'd made a serious mistake, once again underestimating Hackett. The oldest trick in the book – a precaution he would have used himself, indeed had used on several occasions. A wave of self-doubt swept over him, as if the revelations of the grave had drained him not only of his identity but of the expertise he'd once assumed made him one of the best assets in the Service.

Hackett took out a cigarette packet. As his head moved, his glasses cleared. He lit up, releasing smoke from the side of his mouth, all the while keeping his icy blue gaze on Cecil and attempting to conceal the slight tremor in his left eye. 'So you haven't got the film on you.' He leaned back. 'You're a strange man, Cecil. You never cease to intrigue me. I mean, look at yourself, sitting there in those scruffy clothes. Where did you find them? In a clothing bank?' He took another draw on his cigarette and exhaled. 'How the hell did you get Voronov to wear your coat? That was cunning beyond description and quite ruthless in an evil way. It was some time before we realised it wasn't you. And what did you do with the Russians? They've just disappeared. How did you do it?'

Cecil folded his arms, but otherwise kept still.

Hackett changed tack. 'I suppose it's a waste of time having Lessing go over your car, isn't it?'

There was no response.

'Ah well,' he sighed, 'no matter.'

Lessing appeared in the doorway.

'Do come in and join us. Any luck?'

He shook his head. 'No. The car was hired in London but there's nothing in it.'

'As I thought. Pull up a chair and sit here.' Hackett indicated a place on his left before turning back to Cecil. 'Assuming you got hold of the film, what I can't work out is why you came back from London. Was it for Lottie, or is that the romantic in me?'

Cecil remained still, his face expressionless.

Eyes narrowing with the smoke, Hackett leaned forward. 'You need her for something. What is it, I wonder?' He scrubbed out his cigarette on the table-top without any regard for the surface. 'And if you need her, you probably brought the film from London with you. The two go together, don't they, the film and her? Except it's not on you and it's not in the car.'

Cecil unfolded his arms and rested his hands on the table, one on top of the other, glanced up at the ceiling and then turned his gaze back on Hackett.

Uneasy with Cecil's attitude, he tried another approach. 'You've caused the death of three people. In the eyes of the police that's serious, *really* serious. However, we are a deniable unit and if I have the film in my hand, all that can be set aside, just as the shooting in the village was. I don't need to explain the details to you. They wandered into the bog when you were all chasing Voronov. His death?

Well, there was an exchange of fire. Our people will carry out the post-mortems, as you know. The record will show that you located the film, retrieved it and handed it over. You'll be released from duty with much acclaim.'

Cecil leaned toward Hackett. 'Those deaths in the bog and at the coffee bar were self-defence, as you know well. It was you who had Voronov shot, and with a bullet that was meant for me.'

'Well, you had put yourself in an impossible situation.' Hackett rested his elbows on the arms of his chair, confident of his position.

'And Lottie,' Cecil went on, 'how will you gain her silence?'

'You know, I'm still not sure how you feel about her.' He looked at Cecil keenly. 'She's still in our organisation. We can control her. Be assured of that.'

Cecil didn't believe Hackett, no matter how persuasive his offer sounded. Things had gone too far for that. *There's only one way open for him. To persuade me to reveal where the film is by some means or other and to eliminate me, and probably Lottie. I have to move the action out of the house and lure them away from where I've cached the film. Somewhere where their advantage of numbers can be reduced . . . The aqueduct! It would give me a slim chance, if I can convince Hackett I'm willing to do a deal, but it won't be easy. If I give in too quickly, Hackett's suspicions will be raised. I have to be prepared to do whatever it takes. I have no choice. Once the film is out in the open there'll be no consequences.*

Cecil folded his arms again and leaned back on the chair. 'You don't really expect me to believe you would stick to any agreement once you got your hands on the film, do you? The best thing you can do is to let us both walk out of here and hope, when I get that stuff in the public domain, I don't mention what you have been up to in your attempt to suppress it.'

Hackett affected a sigh. 'Oh dear. I *was* hoping we could avoid this. I really don't like violence, especially against women.'

Cecil tensed with a cold fear for Lottie. 'She doesn't know where it is.'

'Yes, I do believe that's true, but surely she knows why you came back. We both know she can be persuaded to tell us and so can

155

you – eventually. Either she's just another pawn that you're prepared to sacrifice in a gambit, or you have something nobler in mind.' He leaned back. 'We shall see. Either way, you'll get a demonstration of what's in store for you.' Hackett stood up placed his fingertips on the table and leaned his face close in an almost psychotic stare. 'Come on, Cecil, you've been through this before. Do you think you can stand up to it again? We both know you'll crack. Everyone does eventually.' He moved his face even closer. 'And how will it leave you this time? Probably having to have your next meal fed to you with a spoon.' He sat down again. 'We're not heroes, Cecil, none of us. This is not an age of heroes.'

Cecil leaned over the table, this time bringing his face close to Hackett's. He spat, 'Go to hell.'

'You're a fool, Cecil.' Hackett turned away. 'Make some preparations, Mr Lessing. That piano bench will do. Bring it away from the window.' Turning back to Cecil, he took out his pistol and pointed it at him. 'Don't do anything silly, like trying to speak to her. Just sit back and enjoy it. Anything else and you get it in the knee.'

Cecil winced.

Lessing went over to the window swept the music sheets off the bench and placed it closer to the table. He used two books of similar thickness to raise one end. Then he went into the kitchen where they heard him moving around and water being run into a vessel of some sort. He came out with a small towel and a large plastic jug which he placed on the table, taking care not to slop the contents. Folding the towel into a flat strip, he laid it beside the jug with the sort of care that comes with the anticipation of enjoyment. He took out a length of cord and tied a slip knot to one end and stuffed it in his pocket. It was all done quickly with practised precision, just as Cecil had anticipated. He wondered desperately how long he should hold out before affecting to crack. He was sickened by the memories set off by the preparations he was witnessing but also surprised to realise he was concerned to spare Lottie as much as possible.

'That's it.' Hackett nodded to express his satisfaction. 'I think we're ready for her now. Bring her down, Lessing.' He turned to Kerr. 'Get ready.' All eyes were turned on the door.

Lottie had been sitting on a hard chair in her bathroom for what seemed an age. *What are they doing to Huw?* She became aware that she was wringing her hands, and that the short gasping breaths she could hear were hers. There were footsteps on the stairs. *Shall I charge at him when he opens the door? Take him by surprise? I could do it. I'm as heavy as him. I could seize his gun. Then what? I wouldn't know how to use it, and they will still have Huw . . .*

The bathroom door was unlocked. Lessing pushed it open and stood back cautiously. He held out his hand. There was no gun. With a smile that was almost a smirk he said, 'Come along. We'd like to speak to you downstairs.'

Chapter Forty-Five

Lottie appeared, with Lessing behind her. As they entered the room he seized her arms, pushed her towards the bench and spun her round. She screamed as both he and Kerr forced her back onto it with her head to the lowered end. In a flash, Lessing slipped the cord around her wrist and passed it under the bench to Kerr. He drew it tight and fastened it so that her back was held against the bench and her wrists pinioned together. At the same time, he took the other cord, secured her ankles and tied them to the bench. Before Lottie could make another sound, Lessing held the folded towel in both hands and forced it tight around her mouth and nostrils, putting all his weight on it so she could only make muffled sounds of outrage. She attempted to twist and turn, urgently sucking air through the fabric into her expanding lungs, then collapsing them as she forced it out to take each panicked breath. The leer in Lessing's eyes set Cecil's teeth on edge. Clearly he was enjoying it. It was all Cecil could do to resist the urge to lunge at him, but no, he must stay his hand for the time being at least.

Unable to watch what he knew was coming next, Cecil turned his head away. Lessing took the jug and, holding it over Lottie's mouth at table height, gently slopped the water onto the towel. Lottie attempted to hold her breath until she was forced to inhale, bringing the damp cloth tight against her nostrils and mouth.

She was overwhelmed by terror. As she started to drown, Cecil heard her involuntarily convulsing and frenziedly writhing. Kerr continued to force her jerking and twisting head down against the bench with all the force he could muster as her back arched and her limbs contorted against the bindings. After ten or twelve seconds Cecil knew, without having to look, that Kerr had removed the towel, for he heard the deep hollow gasp of Lottie's lungs as they drew in air. Unable to avoid it, Cecil turned his head to look. Concerned only with survival, she was left panting, her body shuddering.

'Well, Cecil, what do you think of that?' Hackett turned to him. He hoped this business wouldn't go on much longer. In truth, he had an aversion to violence of any sort. He found it abhorrent, the sort of thing people like Cecil seemed to be good at. But he was desperate. The idea of failure haunted him. He must succeed at this case and he would do whatever was necessary, without regard for procedure. After all, this wasn't classed as torture. He'd put Kerr in his place on that, but he would have to keep an eye on him all the same. These thoughts were pushed to the back of his mind. 'You know, old boy, you can stop this. Just say the word.'

Cecil's face remained set as he looked away from the bench. *How many more times can I let Lottie's ordeal go on? It has to be long enough so that, when I give in, it will seem genuine.*

Hackett turned back to the bench. 'Again, Mr Kerr.'

'Are you sure, sir? I know it doesn't leave marks but . . .'

Hackett voiced his impatience. 'But what, Kerr?'

'They're not the same after, sir, are they? I mean go too far and . . . well . . . anyone can see something bad has happened to them.'

'Get on with it, man. How many times do I have to tell you? I'll take full responsibility.'

So, Cecil thought, *Hackett has no authorisation for this. He must have the phones switched off, closing down Central Control's monitoring.*

The towel was forced down on the lower part of Lottie's face and Lessing stepped forward with the jug. In vain, she attempted to twist her head from side to side, her eyes rolling in fear. This time, Cecil was drawn to look, finding it impossible to maintain his detached stance.

Lessing splashed once, almost playfully, to produce convulsions before the towel was lifted long enough for Lottie to make one drawn-out gasp. It was applied again, brutally forcing her head back against the bench as her body thrashed from side to side. She produced animal-like sounds, muffled by the towel. At the second splash, she stopped breathing altogether. She felt a great pressure as if her whole body might explode. Her tongue felt as if it might fill her mouth, as it seemed to swell and she heard the sound of blood pounding in her ears. She knew she was dying. As she was about to pass out, the towel was lifted.

It was at the third splash of the water that Cecil found he could take no more, almost blinded by rage and increasing remorse at putting her through such terror, he rose to his feet as if compelled. His hands straining at the cuffs he cried, 'Stop!'

Kerr relaxed the pressure immediately and turned to Hackett. Lessing stood aside and they all looked at Lottie, her starved lungs almost bursting as she sucked in air.

'That's enough,' Cecil snarled through gritted teeth, 'She's had enough. So have I. I'll take the deal you offered.'

Hackett turned to him, a note of triumph in his voice . . . or was it relief? 'Sit down Cecil. I'll decide whether it's enough.' Had Cecil given in suspiciously early? 'Does this mean we're going to get the film?'

'Yes, if the offer still stands.'

'Of course. If you'd accepted in the first place, this nastiness could've been avoided. You've only got yourself to blame, you know, old boy. I told you this is not an age of heroes. I suppose you thought you'd act tough, as long as it was someone else taking the unpleasantness. And the reason you came back: what part does she play in that? If I'm not satisfied with your answer, we'll have to put the question to her and continue like this until she answers it.'

Cecil entreated, 'Can't you see she's not fit to answer anything right now?'

'Possibly – but then it will have to be your turn won't it?'

'Untie her and get her off that bench before I say any more.'

Hackett nodded to Kerr who quickly set about releasing Lottie's wrists and ankles with the reluctant help of Lessing. Taking an arm each they attempted to lift her up but her legs gave way. With some difficulty they took her, with feet dragging out of her shoes, to collapse into an armchair. Her head was lolling from side to side and she was panting open-mouthed in distress.

Hackett leaned toward Cecil looking at him intensely. 'Now, old boy, if I'm not satisfied with what you tell me she goes straight back on that bench for another spell and we both know how it will leave her. Then it will be your turn. So,' He leaned back, 'make sure I can believe what I hear.'

Cecil told him about Lottie's role in the local library and how she had access to digitising equipment and what they planned to do when he came back with the film. Hackett listened and sat pondering for a while.

Meanwhile, Cecil's mind was working intensely. The idea of the aqueduct: it might just work. *If I can convince Hackett, it'll get at least two of them in the open, away from the house and the film, to a situation where I'm familiar enough to shift the balance in my favour.*

Hackett broke his silence. 'It's a fascinating explanation, so simple, using the public library. Whether it's true or not is another matter . . . but that has no bearing on the situation right now. Where's the film?'

'There's an aqueduct near here. It carries a canal across a deep valley over the river. On my way up, I stopped, went onto it and hid the film. It's in a waterproof package.'

'You hid the package on this aqueduct – how?' Hackett turned to the other two as if to test for credibility.

'I spotted this aqueduct on the way over here from Oswestry,' Kerr offered. 'It's high, bloody high. Did you two notice it?'

They both shook their heads.

Hackett turned back to Cecil. 'Well?'

'It's in the trough at the middle of the aqueduct, hanging below the water in a waterproof bag. The towpath shelves out about a metre over the water. I leaned out and hung it underneath, hooking it on a girder support. You'll need me to show you. It's a sensitive area; World Heritage Site, visitor centre, and all that. In daytime, from about ten o'clock, especially this time of year, it's busy with people walking on the towpath and boats crossing. I had to wait a while until both ends of the aqueduct were clear. It's best to go in darkness when there'll be nobody about to wonder what a group of men are doing poking around in the water.'

Hackett looked at him piercingly. 'Why do we need you to show us? Just tell us where to find it.'

Cecil racked his brains for a convincing reason. *Think, quickly.* 'There's a chance you would eventually find it without me, I suppose, but it would take a long time, even if you followed my directions closely. Much longer than having me go straight to it. The longer it takes, the more chance of attracting attention.'

Hackett lit another cigarette. Then, after slowly releasing smoke out of the corner of his mouth, all the while keeping his eyes on Cecil, he said, 'I wondered why you took so long getting here after we located your call on the A5 but tell me, why go to such trouble to hide it when you could have brought it straight here?' He took another draw on the cigarette. 'Ah, I see it now. You were warned, weren't you? Somehow you knew we'd be here. You were going to blow us to hell when we opened the door but you weren't counting on Kerr coming up behind you. Another mistake, Cecil, old boy. You really have lost your touch. Though I must say, hiding the stuff where you did, if it is where you say it is, and it had better be there, is inspired though slightly eccentric. Who else but you would have thought of it? It would never have been found.' He stubbed his cigarette out. 'You know, Cecil, I'm going to miss you when you're kicked out of the Service. Just for the record, *did* she warn you somehow?'

Cecil's face remained set.

'Yes, it was something she said wasn't it? Something over the phone. An old trick. I should have realised. Serves me right for

162

being so naïve.' Hackett sat for a moment, his mind turning over. 'How long will it take to get there?'

'About half an hour,' Cecil answered.

'I'm asking Kerr, not you,' Hackett snapped back.

He turned to Kerr who nodded. 'Yes, about that.'

Hackett could feel the film within his grasp. The chance to redeem himself lay before him. *Cecil may be up to something. I can't trust him but, what the hell. I can afford to take a risk. After all, if Cecil is leading me on, I can always return to other means of persuasion so long as I keep hold of him.*

The idea of leaving Cecil behind with Kerr or Lessing made Hackett feel uneasy. It could be dangerous. On the other hand, leaving Cecil with both meant he would have to go it alone. That made him feel uneasy too and he wasn't going to send just one of them, or call for assistance from Oswestry, because he had to find the film himself. There must be no doubt in the ultimate report it was he and he alone that secured the film. Besides, at this stage, he didn't want to explain how Cecil came to reveal the film's whereabouts. That's it; he would take Cecil with him and Lessing, for he would be more reliable than Kerr if things got rough. Kerr seemed to be getting jittery, so he would leave him in charge of the woman and out of the action. But he would get Lessing to leave his phone with him, as would he. Better not to reveal their movements at this stage. What Control doesn't know won't upset them.

Wishing to put on a decisive manner, he stated, 'All right! We'll give it a try. There's some hours of darkness yet.' He turned to Cecil. 'Should it be a problem?'

Cecil shook his head. 'No.'

'Then we'll go now.' Hackett turned to Lessing. 'You'll come with me and you, Kerr, will stay here with the woman, keeping her under guard in the bathroom, of course. One of us will give you a hand getting her up the stairs.' He turned to Lessing, 'I think it best that we leave our phones with Kerr. We don't want the opposition following our movements, do we?'

Lessing hesitated momentarily before handing his phone over.

'Don't worry, he'll break radio silence and contact the Duty Officer at Oswestry if we're not back within a couple of hours. She'll know what to do.'

This confirmed it for Cecil. Control was not aware of what was going on. Hackett was acting on his own, as was he.

Hackett addressed Lessing again, 'Here's Cecil's keys. You're driving. There's a torch in my car.'

Chapter Forty-Six

By the time Lottie was returned to the bathroom, the pain in her lungs was easing but it still left her reluctant to inhale fully, so she kept her breathing shallow. The light had been left off. When she moved to get up and switch it on she was overwhelmed by dizziness and fell back on the chair, but she found it impossible to sit on it without slumping to the floor. And that was when she must have passed out.

She came round, awakened by pains all over. She could feel her back was badly bruised. There were welts on her wrists and ankles, with pins and needles in her arms and an uncontrollable shaking. It was as if she was enveloped in a deep cold. With some caution, she picked herself up and, overcome by a wave of nausea, lurched to the toilet pan, retching painfully. She lowered herself gingerly onto the chair, feeling sore everywhere. Memories of the past few hours surfaced and she began putting things together in her mind.

What was Huw up to? She was torn between gratitude for halting the dreadful process and anger for putting her through it in the first place. Mystified, she asked herself why he had done it. She had barely been able to follow what was said while she was recovering in the chair. Oswestry was mentioned. *So that's where I was taken. Has he really hidden the film on the aqueduct? And why did he give in before he was tortured himself? Was it for my sake or was he willing to sacrifice me for his own ends?* She'd heard them going off before she passed out. That left only Kerr in the house. Where would it all lead? More than anything she wondered what was going to happen to her.

Chapter Forty-Seven

Lessing bundled Cecil into the back of the car while Hackett opened the passenger door. Picking up Cecil's bag, he tossed it in the back before getting in. Then he covered him from the passenger seat with his pistol. Lessing got in the driver's side and they moved off.

They travelled south for twenty-five minutes. Then, under Cecil's guidance, Lessing pulled up in the lane that gave access to the rough track leading up onto the canal mooring basin.

Hackett and Lessing stumbled along in the dark with pistols drawn. Although he had a torch, Hackett was reluctant to use it. Night birds stirred as twigs snapped underfoot. The distant sound of the river cascading over the rapids rose up from the valley to meet them. Suddenly there was a break in the clouds and their way was lit by a huge pale moon painting the world white, so that things came alive in sharp contrast. As they approached the mooring basin, Cecil held his manacled wrists to Hackett. 'I'll need to have these off before I can get up on to the towpath.'

'Really, Cecil, do you think I'll fall for that? We'll drag you up if we have to. Come on.' They seized an arm each and pulled Cecil onto the path, leaving him to sprawl face-down on the gravel. Ignoring the sickening surge of pain in his knee, he struggled to his feet, scattering pebbles into the water, making the moon's reflection leap and sway.

'Now,' Hackett snarled, 'where is it?'

'It's underneath the towpath, in the middle of the aqueduct, as I said before.'

Hackett moved toward Cecil, aiming his gun at him menacingly. 'Explain.'

Cecil indicated with his cuffed hands. 'The path projects over the canal trough. The bag is hanging below the water on a line hooked to a support under it.'

For a split second Hackett paused, as if deciding once more whether to overcome his doubts, whether to believe the film was there and that redemption was within his grasp somewhere on this canal. 'You go ahead and lead us to it. Just remember, you've got two guns pointing at you, so don't try any funny stuff.'

The canal water lay before them gleaming in the moonlight, making it seem an unsupported ribbon floating high above the foaming white water below. The black elongated shadow of the aqueduct pillars extended along the valley, creating a sense of unreality that seemed to hang over the group.

'You first.' Hackett's voice, half command half plea, raised a wry thought in Cecil. *So, he finds the path unsettling, does he? Well, many people did. That's a good thing but how to exploit it?*

The sound of the river was increasing as they neared the mid-point. Hackett raised his voice, 'How much further?' He was beginning to have doubts about the wisdom of coming out there. *Was it such a good idea? Coming this far out, just the three of us? No knowing what Cecil might do as we get closer to the package, but once I get my hands on it, once that's done . . . well, many influential people will be grateful to me. My reputation will be restored, my standing with the family, the Service . . .*

'Almost there now.' Cecil's shout interrupted his stream of thought.

'We'd better be. Otherwise I'll begin to think you're leading us on.' Hackett's suspicions were increasing. He was becoming more nervous and tense.

This will have to be it, Cecil thought. *I daren't string them out any longer.* They were at the middle of the aqueduct, the highest point over the river below. The noise was almost deafening. Cecil stopped and waited until they closed up to him. Pointing down, he called above the sound of the torrent, 'It's below here. I can't manage with these cuffs on, so one of you is going to have to lie out on the path and hang under to get it.' *That will get at least one of them out of the way*, he thought.

Hackett looked at the smooth black water of the canal and gave an inward shudder. 'Oh no, Cecil,' he yelled. 'You're the one who does things like that. Lessing will take off one cuff. You can get down.'

Christ. What do I do now? Cecil felt a surge of panic. It was not going well. Hackett took out the key and passed it to Lessing. Then he came up to the edge. Cocking his pistol, he worked the slide and placed the muzzle at Cecil's ear. Lessing holstered his pistol, took Cecil's wrist, unlocked the cuff and swiftly stepped back, pocketing the key and drawing his gun. Reluctantly, Cecil got down and lay out hanging face down over the side.

Hackett placed a foot in the small of his back and forced him down hard. 'Now get under there. You don't come back up without the package.'

A school of iridescent clouds drifted across the face of the moon, cloaking the valley in long black shadows and immersing the canal in a hoary light. Lying face down under the pressure of Hackett's foot, incensed by the indignity and humiliation, Cecil held out his hand, looking at Hackett's pale reflection on the glass-smooth surface of the water. 'Give me the torch.'

Hackett lifted his foot and gingerly held the torch out. Now was his chance. Cecil twisted round and, sitting up, made a grab for Hackett's torch and the gun in his other hand, intending to swing him round as a shield between Lessing. Hackett let the torch go, springing up and snatching his gun hand free, leaving Cecil to fall backwards into the canal.

He surfaced immediately, shocked by the sudden chill. Floundering, he fell on his backside with the water up to his chest, his shoulder blades pressed painfully against the opposite side of the trough.

Hackett raised his pistol, pointing it at Cecil while replacing his dislodged glasses, hanging from one ear, with a trembling hand. As if detached from the reality of the moment, Cecil found himself still clutching the torch. *This is it. The end of the line.*

'Sir!' Lessing cried above the thunder of the water gently pushing Hackett's gun hand down. 'No need to do that just now, sir.'

Quivering with fury, Hackett turned his face to him. For a moment, Lessing was taken aback by his twitching eye alight with outrage at Cecil's attempted attack. He saw for the first time how possessed with the mission his boss was. Recovering his self-composure, Hackett called to Cecil, 'Try the torch. Does it work?' It did. Gesturing with the pistol he ordered, 'Get under there, but first . . .' He pointed his pistol down at the towpath and fired. Lessing shouted with surprise. For a moment it seemed to Cecil there had been no sound, just a numbness in his ear drums as they flattened with the sudden pressure of the report. He heard Hackett's voice faintly above the sound of the water. 'The round goes straight through the path, so if you try anything while you're under, there'll be no cover.'

One thought clouded the elation following Cecil's respite: what to do now? Warm summers flashed before his mind's eye, with him and his friends floating on their backs in the dark water of the canal, pulling themselves along by the iron lattice-work. *Can I do it now? Can I distract them somehow and lure them away, so I can move under the towpath in the opposite direction? It's my only chance.* Wading to the edge of the towpath, he ducked under. Once underneath, he splashed with his feet as if he was attempting to run, hoping they would hear over the noise of the river. Then he threw the torch as hard as possible towards the mooring basin from where they had come so that it struck the ironwork. The loud clang rang above the sound of the river below.

'The bastard's making a run for it!' Hackett bellowed. He fired two random shots in the direction of the sound. Spinning round to Lessing, he shouted, 'See if you can take him alive!' Lessing made off at a run, leaving Hackett to peer into the gloom after him.

Cecil was desolate. They'd split up. The decoy plan had failed. The situation seemed hopeless. In sheer terror, he ducked under the water and crawled out from the path. Coiling himself, he sprang, lunging for Hackett's ankles and, seizing them, he fell back into the canal pulling him in with him. Rolling over like a striking alligator, he surfaced on top of Hackett, trying to hold him under the water with all the frenzied strength he could muster. It was in vain, the handcuffs dangling from one wrist hampering him, allowing Hackett to wriggle free.

Hackett raised his gun, but too late. Cecil flailed at it with the cuffed wrist, sending it flying – but in so doing, sprawling himself forwards under the water. The gun landed somewhere along the path. Hackett seized his chance. Scrambling onto the path after it, he staggered to his feet, leaving his glasses behind. Cecil recovered, thrashing through the water after him, attempting in vain to seize his leg as he hauled himself out, forcing Hackett to turn back. He launched himself at Cecil with such force that only his shoulders striking the bars of the railings stopped him plunging through into the void. Hackett was on him, his hands scrabbling for a hold on his throat and pushing him through the gap between the bars. Cecil grasped one bar and, desperately attempting to use the cuff as a flail, lashed out, hitting the back of Hackett's head. There was just enough force to loosen his hold, so that Cecil twisted out of his grip, coming up behind him. He forced Hackett round so they were face-to-face. A renewed strength fired by an overwhelming desire for vengeance arose in him. Now he would avenge Lottie's torture and atone for his part in bringing it about. He knew what he was going to do. This was familiar territory. Hackett went for his throat again. Cecil ducked down bringing their heads below the cross bar of the railing and twisting Hackett's shoulders through. Bracing himself against the top bar, he gently nudged Hackett with his chest, just enough to avoid being dragged through by his weight. The man was left clasping Cecil's neck with both hands as he hung out over the foaming river far below. His feet scrabbled in vain for a hold on the cast-iron trough. His pale blue eyes fixed on Cecil as if pleading, 'Help me,' he said. But there was no salvation for him. Cecil wrenched Hackett's hands from his neck and watched him as he fell back into space with a wail of despair.

170

With no time to react, Cecil scurried along the path bent double and fumbling for Hackett's gun until he found it. It was a standard issue Glock.

Lessing had reached the spot where he judged Cecil to be and was about to lie out and peer under the path, when he heard the disturbance and turned to see the desperate struggle. Unable to distinguish the scuffling bodies in the poor light, he cocked his pistol as he ran, firing once over their heads in an attempt to distract them. Getting closer he saw one body fall. By the time he realised who it was, Cecil had picked up Hackett's gun and was levelling it at him. Lessing slowed down to a walk.

Panting for breath Cecil was shivering with the clinging dampness of his wet clothes and the chill of the early morning air. Lessing's eyes were drawn to the tremor in his gun hand. He perceived he was jittery and dangerous. The scene brought him to a stop. They were less than three metres apart, face-to-face, with weapons pointed at each other.

Chapter Forty-Eight

The air between Cecil and Lessing crackled with tension. The sound of the river was behind them now. After a taut silence, Lessing spoke in a voice hoarse with nervousness, 'It's not here, is it?' He sounded resigned, almost fatalistic, as if he'd never expected anything different.

Cecil nodded in acknowledgement.

'You'd have done for me as well as him, if you'd had a chance. That's why you led us here. To get us out on this bloody bridge and tackle us one by one. Well, it hasn't worked out, has it?'

Cecil was trembling so much it was difficult for him to speak. For a fraction of a second, his eyes flickered over the valley and back. There was a thin band of yellow and orange on the horizon, widening against a lightening sky.

Over Lessing's shoulder, something was moving. It was a narrow boat silently emerging from the mooring basin. Barely visible in the pink-tinted twilight of early morning, it was making its slow approach onto the aqueduct. Striving to keep his face blank and avoid registering what he could see, Cecil's mind churned. How best to take advantage of the distraction that would occur as Lessing became conscious of the boat behind him. 'It's getting light,' he managed to say through chattering teeth. Then he grasped the pistol with both hands, grimly tightening his trembling grip on it and all the while conscious of the loose cuff dangling from his wrist. 'What do we do – or what do you do?' *Keep talking*, his mind told him, *dampen the sound of the engine as long as possible.*

Now he could see a figure at the stern of the longboat, a man holding the tiller, and there was another appearing from the cabin. The boat came nearer. *How much longer can I keep masking the sound*, Cecil thought, while desperately trying to hold Lessing's attention with his eyes. Lessing turned as he picked up the engine's low chugging and the rustling of the displaced water.

There was the crack of a gunshot. It reverberated down the valley. A murder of crows rose from the trees lining the river bank, soaring over the river, cawing their raucous complaint far and wide. Lessing had fallen forward onto the towpath.

Almost at the same instant, a second shot rang out as Cecil turned to the source of the first, squeezing his trigger in reaction. The man slumped half over the side of the boat, his gun clattering onto the deck. The other man let go of the tiller, springing to his feet and fumbling desperately for his gun but Cecil had time to take careful aim. The bullet took the man in the chest, hurling him backwards to hang over the stern, his legs trapped by the tiller, his head submerged. With a sputter, the boat's engine cut.

Cecil stood almost convulsing with shock and the chill of his wet clothes, his eyes fixed on the narrow boat as it slid past under its own momentum. Then he shook himself mentally. *The keys*, he thought. Rolling Lessing's corpse over on its back, he tore at the jacket, rummaging in the pockets and rootling them out. With a grunt of satisfaction, he unlocked the cuff and freed his wrist as he tottered and stumbled his way down the path to the car.

Snatching open the door, he pulled out the bag and emptied its contents. Casting off his sodden clothes, he paused momentarily to let the keen morning air dry his skin before dressing. He felt the suffusing warmth as he fastened his jacket over the shoulder holster.

He was himself again.

Chapter Forty-Nine

Kerr smoked his last cigarette. It was well over two hours since they'd left and no contact of any kind. Now it was beginning to seem that splitting up had been the wrong thing to do. A feeling of unease settled upon him. It was time to break the silence, he thought. But there would be some awkward questions and some explaining. *I can't leave it any longer. They're not coming back. The longer I leave it, the more awkward it's going to be. What the hell am I going to tell them? Once I make that call, everything'll kick off. I'd better get the woman down, otherwise . . . otherwise it won't look good with her locked up, especially as I might be left to explain what happened to her. I was only doing what I was told. Perhaps she'll vouch for me. I did question it. Yes that's it, I'll get her down, try and soften her up, get her to see things from my side. Then I'll call Oswestry.*

Lottie had lost sense of time. Her condition had worsened. She was passing in and out of consciousness, occasionally staggering to the wash bowl to slake a raging thirst from the tap. As if from a distance, she became aware of movement. There was Kerr standing at the open door, somehow out of focus. How long had he been there? She didn't know.

He came toward her. 'You're coming down where you'll be more comfortable.' He held out his hand. 'Let me take your arm.' He attempted to hold her around the waist but her weight made it difficult for him. Struggling and almost carrying her step by step down the stairs to the living room, he settled her into one of the easy chairs. 'I'll get you some tea,' she heard him say as if from afar. Then he was gone. He was moving about somewhere. Was it in the kitchen? Then she was holding a mug. The tea was hot and sweet. It warmed her. She could feel it coursing through, clearing the dizziness and steadying her breathing. Now she could see him more clearly. He was sitting opposite, leaning toward her. Where was his gun? It must be on him somewhere. She would try and concentrate.

'I'm very sorry about what happened earlier,' he said. 'Can you understand what I'm saying?' She must have given some sign, a movement of her head perhaps, because he went on, 'If you remember – I did what I could to stop it – short of using force.'

What was he talking about? Lottie shifted in her chair. Sensation was back and with it emotion, shock, fear giving way to recall. Her head was clearing. She was coming to.

Kerr took out his phone. 'You're not fit to go yet. I'm going to call Oswestry, tell them what's happened, to get you some medical help and let them take it from there.'

He keyed in the call.

Chapter Fifty

The control room door at Oswestry, swollen with damp, briefly resisted the Duty Officer's impatient shove, doing nothing to improve her unease as she came into the room. She addressed her assistant curtly, 'Any change?'

'No, ma'am. No change. Not since the Boss sent the technician back and the phones were switched off soon after. He's still not responding and they've not moved from the house.'

'According to the phones, that is.'

'Yes, ma'am.'

Shit, she thought. *This* would *happen on my watch. Something's wrong, very wrong.* This was the first time she'd been left in command since her appointment to this post two months before.

'And there's no other way of contacting them, apart from actually going there?'

'No, ma'am. There's no landline and we have her laptop here.'

'We're going to have to get over there. Call the Office and report the situation to—' The main telephone rang stridently, tightening her nerves. Snatching it up, she held it for some moments. 'Wait,' she snapped at her assistant. As she listened to Kerr, she tensed then demanded, 'Location of this aqueduct?' She noted it down. 'I'll get everyone available over to it. Meanwhile Cecil may be on his way to you. You're on your own 'til I can get someone over. Is that clear?' She placed the receiver down, pausing – she was collected now. This was what the job was about. She turned to her assistant. 'Did you hear that?'

'Yes, ma'am. What about the local Special Branch, do we bring them in?'

'With the boss out of it at the moment, it'll have to be referred to the Main Office. I expect they'll want them kept out until we know what's happened. I'll get to this aqueduct with everyone that can be spared. Make a note of the location then get that information to the office and follow on after me.'

Chapter Fifty-One

At the aqueduct

The Duty Officer's assistant pulled over as he spotted one of his men on the footpath and leapt out of the car, bounding over to him.

'Where is she?'

'Up there on the towpath. It's not looking good.'

The Duty Officer was standing over Lessing's body. There were two men at her side and the assistant was conscious of more moving about behind him. She nodded toward the mooring basin. 'It looks as if Cecil's been busy. There's two more over there. On a boat, Russians. And where the hell is the boss?'

The assistant stared down at Lessing for some moments before looking up. 'Thames House are in agreement. Hold off on the Specials until they know more, they said.'

The Duty Officer murmured something in acknowledgement. 'We'll have to get the local uniforms in, though. There'll be people about soon. Take over with that. You know what to do. Same as before at the village.'

Chapter Fifty-Two

Once more, Cecil pulled up in the lane beside the old pit-bank and cautiously climbed up to his former observation position. The hiding place was undisturbed. Lottie's house seemed quiet, no cars, nothing to be seen. It was possible Kerr hadn't contacted Oswestry but, on the other hand, they could be on their way. If so, they would arrive at any moment. There was no time to lose. How best to approach the house with Kerr most likely on watch upstairs and Lottie still locked in the bathroom? There was only one way for it.

Cecil drove the car down the main road from the west as fast as driving conditions allowed. As it approached Lottie's drive, a handbrake turn swung it round at ninety degrees to screech up the drive, stopping behind her vehicle. He sprang out, using both cars as cover. Half limping, half running, he made it to the front door. The lock was demolished with one shot. He expected this would draw Kerr down to the front of the house. Then he stumbled to the side gate and, with a fierce, shoulder-bruising charge, it flew open. Next it was the side door. Shooting out the lock, he kicked it open.

Kerr was waiting for him, pistol levelled.

Chapter Fifty-Three

'Drop it.'

Cecil complied.

'Hands on your head.'

He had no choice.

Using his pistol, Kerr gestured to the living room. 'Get in there.'

Lottie was standing against the window, startled, her heart pounding. She'd risen to her feet as the shots rang out one after another. Kerr herded Cecil into the room keeping a careful distance. He took a dining chair and placed it to face the corner opposite Lottie. 'Sit down, keep your face to the wall, hands on your head. Anything else and I fire.'

Cecil's eyes met hers as he turned to face the corner. They seemed to convey an intensity that dispelled her feelings of helplessness, giving her hope.

Turning his head slightly, Kerr spoke to her over his shoulder, while keeping his eyes on Cecil, 'I'm going to have to insist you sit down and stay exactly where you are. It won't be for long. The others will be here soon and then it will all be over.' He addressed Cecil, 'You can put your hands down,' and started towards him raising his pistol to strike his head.

He's going to hit him. Lottie was horrified. 'No!' Cecil heard her scream half in anger, half in terror.

Distracted for a moment, Kerr turned his head. Lottie seized her chance and launched herself at him. Kerr recovered, but too late – she was on him, with her full weight setting him back. She scrabbled for the gun as he tried to shake her off, grappling him around the waist with her free hand and using her mass to push him toward the wall. They collided with Cecil, hurling him forward so that his head struck the wall, briefly stunning him.

At the same time, she sank her teeth into Kerr's nose. Desperately, he grabbed a handful of red hair, wrenching her head back in a spray of his own blood, attempting to bring his gun hand up to her head just as she swung him around. There was a loud bang. Kerr sagged in Lottie's arms and dropped to the floor, leaving the gun in her hand. She stood looking down at the crumpled body, still holding the pistol, her panicked breath coming in short gasps.

Cecil was on his knees. As his head cleared, he got to his feet. Carefully he circled round, slowly coming into the margin of her vision. Quietly, he spoke her name. There was no response. Again, louder this time, 'Lottie.'

Slowly, she turned to him. Hesitating, as if searching for her voice, she said, 'Do you know, I can't hear a thing except this ringing in my ears?'

He put out his hand and took the weapon then, clasping her hands, he pressed them lightly to his lips before saying, 'Come on. We'll get the film and then we'll go to the library.'

His voice was faint and tinny but she understood. Her hearing was coming back. 'What about the mess we've left?'

'Don't worry. It'll be sorted out.'

'I'll have to get my shoes on.'

As they got in the car she asked, 'And Huw Syssel, has he been sorted out?'

'Yes. Yes, I think he has.' There was a pause. 'And Miss Lottie Williams-Parry, what about her?'

'Yes I think she's become the person she could have been all those years ago.'

He leaned over to her and gently placed a kiss on her lips. 'Come on. We've got work to do.'

Chapter Fifty-Four

At a signal from the Duty Officer, six men cautiously entered the house from each door. One of them came to the front and signed for her and her assistant to come in. Since Hackett's body had been found by picnickers, rolling in the shallows three miles downstream of the aqueduct, she was in complete charge, at least for the time being. As she thoughtfully looked over the scene, her assistant said, 'The birds have flown, ma'am. Shall we go after them or call for assistance?'

'Let them go,' she answered. 'We've done all we can.' She stepped into the hall and walked toward the front door, followed by her assistant. Then, on an impulse as if to check, she turned into the front room. Moving to the window, she gently pulled a curtain aside and looked out saying softly, 'The rest is up to others out there now.'

Acknowledgements

I give my thanks to Officer 3564 BOX for his help on techniques and weaponry.

I am also grateful for the encouragement of my partner, Jean Gatheral, who gave me the idea of setting a crucial scene on the Pontcysyllte Aqueduct which itself became one of the main characters in the novel.